Unfinished Business

A Cozy Mystery

USA TODAY Bestselling Author

Denise Devine

Dedication

To Linda

Chapter One

Mid-August

The flowers, balloons and stuffed bears at the foot of Alana Morgan's front door resembled a shrine for the dead.

With one hand on her suitcase and the other holding her keys, she stood in the hallway outside her condo and stared down at the colorful exhibition in dismay. The display wasn't a memorial for someone. It was for *something*; a relationship with Dylan O'Rourke that should have never happened.

The door of the condo next to hers cracked open a few inches. Gina Alfonsi poked her graying head into the hallway. "He's been here every day this week. Now that you're back home, you need to either kiss and make up or get a restraining order." Shaking her head in disgust, Gina stared at the items piled on the floor. "Put the poor guy out of his misery."

Alana deactivated her security system then put her key in the deadbolt lock and turned it. "We had it out just before I left for Paris and I gave him back the engagement ring. He begged me to forgive him but I refused. A couple nights ago, I described the situation to my girlfriends and they agreed I'd be crazy to take him back." She pushed the door open. "I don't care how sorry Dylan is; he's history. There is *no* second chance for a man who cheats." Leaving her suitcase behind for now, she stepped over the obstacles in her way and entered her condominium.

She would have never known about his infidelity if her business trip to Los Angeles hadn't been cut short. A product manager in retail price management for a private software firm, she'd planned to be in L.A. for five days to work with a client. The meetings, however, were very productive and wrapped up a day early, giving her an extra day to get ready for her trip to Paris. She'd caught the red-eye back to Minneapolis on Thursday night. Arriving home early Friday morning, she'd purchased muffins from a coffee shop and had gone straight to Dylan's place on the sixth floor of her condo complex. She wanted to surprise him before he left for work, but a nasty surprise was in store *for her* when she let herself in and discovered her fiancé in the shower with another woman...

Alana grimaced. *Why do I always manage to pick losers?*

Successful, sexy and sweet-talking, Dylan's charming personality was the kind she always fell for, but obviously, his kind wasn't right *for her*. A relationship had to be based upon more than physical attraction and she realized now theirs had been merely skin-deep. That's why he'd cheated on her. In the end, he'd come to that conclusion too, and that's why he wanted to start over, but it was too late. She could never trust him again.

Alana crossed the living room to the floor-to-ceiling windows and pulled open the fabric blinds, filling her spacious home with afternoon sunlight. She loved living on the thirtieth floor of Marquette Towers. Situated on the south edge of downtown Minneapolis, the spectacular view of the metro area from her balcony stretched as far as she could see. Looking downward, her gaze swept across the lush, eleven-acre grounds of the Sculpture Garden a couple blocks away and Loring Park with tall, shady trees and its centerpiece, Loring Lake. She'd had a great time in Paris, but it was good to be back in Minnesota again.

Well, it would be once she'd returned Dylan O'Rourke's gifts and purged him from her life forever.

Gina stood in the doorway wearing black leggings, a lacy white tunic and a necklace of chunky aqua beads. She smiled, revealing a space between her front teeth. "Did you have a good trip?"

"Oh, yes! I always have a great time with my ex-roommates from college. We take a vacation together every year at the end of the summer for some girls-only fun. It's been our tradition since we graduated."

Alana dropped her purse on the coffee table and began to collect the items in the doorway. The flowers went into the trash. "On our first day, we had lunch at a sidewalk café and spent the afternoon shopping," she said as she poured the water from the vases into the sink. "On other days, we wandered through The Louvre, took a river cruise on the Seine and watched the evening light show at the Eiffel Tower."

"How was the wine?"

"Wonderful!" Alana knelt in front of the doorway holding a white garbage bag in her hands. "One evening we went to a place on Rue des Boulangers where we drank Bordeaux and snacked on wild boar sausage with cheese and crackers." She shoved a stuffed bear into the bag.

Gina laughed. "The wine sounds good. I'm not sure about the wild boar..."

"It wasn't as bad as it sounds. It tasted like summer sausage to me."

As Alana worked, she thought back to that balmy night in Paris. Josie, Ryley, Emma, Annika and she had started confessing their tales of relationships gone bad as they sipped on delicious Bordeaux. By the end of the evening, they'd all promised to hit the "pause" button on love and swear off men for one year so they could focus on pursing their professional goals instead.

Deep in her heart, Alana truly wanted to find Mr. Right, get married and have a couple kids, but for now, the prospect seemed so remote. Were all the good men her age taken? It certainly felt that way. Maybe her friends were right about putting relationships on hold for a while to focus on their careers. The thought of pursuing a high-level promotion at work energized her, giving her a renewed sense of purpose.

"Here, let me help you with that," Gina said as she tucked her chin-length hair behind her ears and knelt on the floor to push a couple Mylar balloons into the bag. They suddenly slipped from Gina's hands and popped out, rocketing toward the ceiling.

"Hold on. I'll fix this." Alana went into the kitchen and grabbed a scissors from one of the drawers. She pulled down the balloons, stabbing a hole in each one and dropping them, deflated, into the bag. She quickly pulled the bag's drawstrings tight and tied them in a knot. "It needs one more thing." She went back into the kitchen to retrieve a note card, a black Sharpie and some cellophane tape. On the card she wrote "Delivery Refused - Return to Sender" and taped it on the bag. "That should do it. I'll go down to the sixth floor and set it in front of *his* door."

Gina folded her arms as she leaned against the door frame. "Judging by how persistent he is, I doubt it will deter him."

Alana set the bag aside with a sigh. "You're right. When he sees the bag, he'll know I'm back and he'll try to talk me into giving our relationship another chance. The problem is, it'll simply be round two of the same argument we've already had. I have nothing else to say to him."

"It's too bad you couldn't go back to Paris for another week."

"I'd love that!" Alana glanced at her suitcase, packed full with new clothes from Paris and she winced at the thought of how much she'd already overspent her travel budget. "Unfortunately, I can't afford to go back there right now. Besides, I called my mom at the airport to let her know my plane had arrived and she talked me into spending the other half of my vacation at my grandmother's house. I'm supposed to start packing Grandma Essie's things and doing some serious cleaning to get the house ready to put on the market."

"You sound like you're dreading it," Gina remarked.

"This isn't my idea of a fun vacation." She looked back at Gina. "My parents rarely ask for my help so I feel duty-bound to set my own plans aside and get the project started for them while they're in Europe celebrating their fortieth anniversary. Grandma Essie's passing took an emotional toll on Mom so she really needs this time away. Well, it was tough on all of us. It's going to be difficult going back there because I have so many memories tied to that house, but I guess I should see the place one last time before it goes up for sale. Growing up, I spent a lot of my summers there and I'm really going to miss it."

It would be a nice change for a few days to wake up in the same bedroom her mother had occupied as a child in Grandma Essie's big house in Merrick. The small, southern Minnesota town was a little boring, perhaps, but at least she'd have some peace and quiet for a few days. Nothing ever happened there…

Until Essie's untimely death.

How? Why? At Mom's Fourth of July picnic, Grandma Essie was her usual self—funny and in good health. She'd lived in that house for sixty years and never had any problem with the back steps. What had caused her to take such a bad fall now? I wish I knew!

Alana shook off the sad, frustrating thoughts. "Why don't you come in for a few minutes, Gina, and visit with me while I repack my suitcase? I'll get you a bottle of sparkling water. I need to get on the road before rush hour starts or it will be a nightmare trying to get out of the metro area. Fridays are always the worst."

After retrieving a couple cold bottles of Voss water from the refrigerator, Alana pulled her suitcase into her bedroom and dumped the contents onto her bed. Gina sat on the corner of her king-sized mattress and chatted with her about Paris as Alana packed enough clothes to stay at Grandma Essie's for a week. When she finished, she went back into her living room and closed the blinds then went into the kitchen and filled out a new index card.

"Enjoy the rest of your vacation," Gina said as she tossed her empty bottle in the recycling bin under the sink. She followed Alana out the door. "If lover boy shows up again, I'll act like I haven't seen you."

"Great, thanks!" Alana locked the door and set the alarm with her key fob. "I'm all set. See you when I get back, Gina!"

Setting her purse on top of her suitcase, Alana took one last look around. "Oops, I almost forgot this…" She held out the notecard with a piece of tape on it and stuck it on the door.

They laughed.

She made her way toward the elevators rolling her suitcase with one hand and dragging Dylan's bag with the other. At the corner, she stopped and looked back to make sure the sign on her door hadn't fallen off. It was still there. The notecard simply read, "Gone Fishing."

***

Reid Sinclair sat at the computer in his home office, working from his notes on a keynote address to be given at a leadership summit in late September. He needed to complete the first draft by the end of the week and send it to his colleague and business partner, Nate Gilbertson, for review. A management professor at the University of Minnesota, Nate critiqued all of Reid's manuscripts, conducted research projects with him and filled the role of agent for Reid's conference schedule and his published books. Reid needed peace and quiet to concentrate, but his private landline phone had been ringing off the hook all day with family and friends calling, grating on his nerves and repeatedly disrupting his concentration.

"Da-dee, the phone is ringing!"

"I know that, Hannah," he replied to his five-year-old daughter who was supposed to be watching a children's show on television. "Just let it go to the answering machine. Daddy will play the messages back later."

"You always say that," she wailed from the living room. "I *like* to answer the phone."

"No, Hannah, let the machine take a message—"

"Hallo?" He suddenly heard her little voice chirp. "Who is this? I'm Hannah and I'm five..." The little pause meant Hannah was nodding at the phone while holding up five fingers. "My da-dee? He's *working*." Another little pause. "Oh-kay!" Little footsteps scampered through the living room to the door of Reid's office. "Da-dee, the lady says you haf to talk to her."

Reid swiveled his chair to see Hannah standing in the doorway with the white cordless phone in her tiny outstretched hand. Instead of becoming angry with her for disobeying him, a twinge of guilt embraced his heart at her sweet, but disheveled appearance. Her white leggings and pink unicorn shirt were stained with the macaroni and cheese she'd spilled on herself at lunch. Her blonde braids were yesterday's hairdo, now coming apart with stray hairs poking out everywhere.

Hannah came into the room and leaned against his knee, her bright blue eyes shining up at him. "Here," she said and offered him the mobile handset. "It's important!"

"Okay, honey," he said as he accepted the phone. "Now you be a good girl and go back into the living room to watch TV. Okay?"

"Who is it?"

"I don't know yet."

"Can I haf a fruit snack?"

Reid nodded, anxious to get her back in front of the TV until he'd finished his call. "But only one. I don't want you to spoil your appetite for dinner."

Hannah beamed. "Oh-kay!"

"What do you say?"

"Thank you!" She turned and ran out of the room.

"Don't—" ...*run in the house*... He shook his head, letting it go for now and hit the speakerphone on the handset. "This is Reid."

"It's Monique."

The clear, feminine sound of his ex-wife's voice startled him. The fingers on his free hand, white-knuckled and tense, gripped the arm of his chair. He hadn't spoken to her in years and their last conversation had been less than friendly. He still remembered every word. Why was she calling him after all this time? His mind swirled with suspicion. "How did you get the private number to my home? It's unlisted." Only a small number of people knew it. One of them had betrayed him.

"It doesn't matter," she replied hastily. "I'm calling to find out how Hannah is doing."

His temper flared. "What do you care? You haven't seen her since the day you abandoned her."

Hannah had just turned three months old when Monique left. Their daughter was registered to start all-day kindergarten in a couple weeks. He was glad Hannah had been too young to remember Monique or recognize her voice on the phone. The less Hannah knew about

Monique, the better.

"Look, Reid, I know you were angry about the divorce. I understand what a shock it was at the time, but that was five years ago. I've had a lot of time to think about the way I acted and I want to make amends."

"I forgive you. Case closed. Don't bother calling again. As soon as I hang up, I'm changing this number."

"Reid," Monique countered in a low, warning voice, "Hannah is my daughter, too, and I want to see her. I want to get to know her and start the proceedings for joint custody."

What the…?

"You've got to be kidding me." He sat ramrod straight, his heart hammering behind his eyes. "Not in a million years would I trust you with her!"

"You can't stop me from seeing my daughter."

"I'll keep you in court for the rest of your life if that's what it takes," Reid snapped. "When my lawyers offered you a fortune to sign away your parental rights, you couldn't wait to put your signature on the agreement to get your hands on the money. You got exactly what you wanted and so did I. There's no going back now."

"I want joint custody of Hannah," Monique repeated acidly. "She's my daughter and I have a right to see her."

Reid had all he could do to keep from throwing the phone on the floor and pulverizing it with his heel, but he kept his voice calm. "Not after what you did. You don't deserve her."

"I knew you'd try to keep me from seeing her. If you persist, I'll go after full custody."

Good luck with that, lady. Any lawyer that got involved in your case would be just taking your money…

He drew in a deep breath. "Look, I still have the security tapes and plenty of evidence to show you're not fit to be Hannah's mother. When she's old enough to understand the situation, I'll let *her* decide if she wants to see you or not. In the meantime, leave us alone. Don't call here *ever* again." Shaking with fury, he ended the call and blocked the number.

"Da-dee," Hannah cried breathlessly as she ran into Reid's office. She pointed to the window. "Someone is at Grandma Essie's house!"

Monique's call had distracted Reid so intensely he could barely concentrate on anything else. He stared at the floor, trying to calm down and wondering what to do now.

Hannah tugged at his sleeve. "Da-dee! Look!"

Reid pulled his thoughts away from the current crisis to gaze out the window at his neighbor's house. The elderly lady had passed away a month ago with a head injury from a bad fall and since then, except for the man who mowed the lawn every week, the house had been ignored.

A car had pulled into the gravel driveway dividing the two properties and it was partially hidden by Essie's white picket fence and giant pink hollyhocks, but he could see enough of it to make out a bright red Mercedes convertible. A tall, slender woman with elbow-length dark hair who looked to be in her early thirties stood next to it, taking in the house and yard. The pricey car, oversized sunglasses and fancy purse on her shoulder gave her a pampered, ultra-feminine look. Someone who was used to having money and expensive tastes—*like Monique.* Even so, he had a hard time pulling his gaze away. Something about the woman caught his eye. The way she leaned against the car, her hands at her sides, staring at the huge red brick, Queen Anne-style house intrigued him. She seemed hesitant…longing for something…

Hannah tugged at his sleeve. "Can we go see her? Pweeease?"

14

He spanned his hands around Hannah's waist and pulled her onto his lap. "Honey, she's probably a realtor who's been contracted to sell the house. If we went over there, we'd just be bothering her. Besides, it's damp outside from the rain and the mosquitoes are really bad today."

Hannah began to cry and rub her eyes with the back of her hands. "I wanna go to Grandma Essie's house!"

Reid slid his arms around her and kissed the top of her head. She'd missed her nap today because he'd been too busy working on his speech to put her in bed with a picture book after lunch and she was clearly overtired. "You miss Grandma Essie, don't you?" he murmured.

Hannah nodded her head and continued to cry.

"I do, too." He wiped her tears away with his thumbs.

Ever since they moved to Merrick ten months ago, Grandma Essie had taken care of Hannah whenever he needed a sitter. She'd even kept Hannah overnight when he had to go out of town on business. The elderly lady had been recommended to him by the Lutheran pastor in town and because of her excellent references, he'd trusted her explicitly. It was an unfortunate accident that had taken her life and he missed her. He didn't know what he was going to do without her.

"Hey," he said in a soft voice and brushed a lock of stray hair from Hannah's face. "Do you want to go to McDonald's and get a Happy Meal for dinner?" He only took her out for fast food on days when his schedule was tight, and give the interruptions he'd had today, he was definitely in no mood to switch gears and cook. He'd print out what he had written so far and review it while Hannah ate her chicken nuggets.

"Oh-kay," Hannah said through her tears.

"But first, go to your room and put on a clean outfit. Then we'll wash your face and brush your hair."

Momentarily appeased, she slid off his lap and ran out of the room.

Reid leaned back in his chair and covered his face with his hands. He didn't know if Monique truly meant what she said about going after him in court, but he couldn't afford to ignore her threat. He needed a plan—and fast. It had cost him nearly everything to get rid of her, including his position as CEO of a nationwide auto parts company. In the years since the divorce, he'd relocated, become a full-time caregiver to his daughter and reinvented himself in the business world.

He took his hands away from his face and stared at the phone. No way would he allow Monique to upend their lives again. *No way...*

Chapter Two

The next morning, Alana awoke in her mother's old bedroom upstairs at Grandma Essie's house; the one with the pink and white flowered wallpaper and matching homemade quilt on the white canopied bed. Ever since she could remember, she'd always slept in this room when visiting her grandma. Rubbing her eyes, she sat up, feeling like a kid again. Outside her window, birds chirped as a light breeze rustled the trees. The house had a familiar, comforting peace about it, as though Grandma Essie was downstairs right now, bustling about the kitchen.

Slipping out of bed, Alana walked over to the bedroom closet and pulled out a white flowered sundress and sandals to wear. She didn't feel like tearing apart dressers and closets today to organize and pack up the remnants of her grandmother's life. She just wanted one more day to enjoy the place as she'd always known it.

The morning sun peeked through the east windows as she slipped into the dress, washed her face in the upstairs bathroom and went downstairs to the spacious kitchen to make a pot of coffee. Yesterday, on her way through Merrick, she'd stopped at the town's only grocery store and stocked up on a few essentials, purchasing enough food for the week

In the summertime, Grandma Essie had always arranged wicker furniture on her wraparound front porch to make a cozy outdoor living room, including a glass-topped table and chairs. She used to love to sit on her porch, drinking coffee and enjoying the beautiful weather. Neighbors walking by would stop to chat. Essie's empty chair by the white balustrade filled Alana's heart with sadness and a wave of nostalgia as she took her coffee and toast outdoors to sit a while.

It's amazing how things I took for granted as a child, I now cherish and have adopted as my own traditions.

She had just eaten the last bite of toast when a neighbor and her lifelong friend, Jemma Bakken, emerged from the front porch of a large house two doors down on the opposite side of the street. Growing up, she and Jemma had formed a special bond because they were both an only child. They'd spent many lazy summers together, swimming, reading and riding their bikes down to the Tip Top Dairy Bar for ice cream.

Once the school year had ended, Alana's parents brought her to Merrick to stay with her grandmother for three months. She had always looked forward to summertime, staying with Grandma Essie and hanging out with Jemma. She had known Jemma for as long as she could remember.

Though she and Jemma were the same age and had many of the same interests, fashion wasn't one of them. She wore the latest designer fashions, whereas Jemma had favored the Bohemian look since she was a teen. Half Scottish and half Czech, Jemma's wild, coppery curls covered her creamy shoulders and arms as she sashayed along the sidewalk carrying a clear plastic container. The short, petite woman wore a long, flowered skirt, a beige, off-shoulder peasant blouse and flat, jeweled sandals. "Hey, there, Alana!" She waved and opened the gate of the white picket fence surrounding the yard. "I brought you a treat for your coffee."

"Is it a box of kolache?" The filled pastries, a local tradition, were Alana's favorite treat. At Jemma's nod, Alana clapped. "Do you remember when we were kids and we snitched a warm apple pie from Mrs. Svoboda's back porch? We got sick from eating the entire thing!"

Jemma laughed as she came through the front gate, leaving it open. "Yeah, but that wasn't as bad as the time we ate hot dogs at the drugstore lunch counter then went to the park and spun around too fast on the merry-go-round."

Alana's palms covered her cheeks. "Oh, my gosh, I'd forgotten about that. It's no wonder I don't like them anymore."

Jemma bounced up the front steps, her metal and beaded bracelets jingling. "How have you been?"

"Great! I've just returned from a week in Paris."

"That's on my bucket list," Jemma said with a sigh as she approached the table. "Did you and Dylan take a romantic river cruise?"

Alana tensed. "No...we broke up just before I left."

"What?" Jemma's moss-green eyes widened in shock. "Why?"

"I caught him cheating on me."

"I'm so sorry," Jemma said as she set the box on the table and gave Alana a hug. "Want to talk about it?"

"Of course. Haven't we always told each other everything?" Alana pushed back her chair and stood. "I'll get the coffee pot first and then I'll fill you in on the details." She disappeared into the house and quickly reappeared with a thermal pot, a small pitcher of cream, a stack of paper napkins and a large mug for Jemma. She filled Jemma's cup then sat down and told her everything, including the conversation she'd had in Paris with her girlfriends about putting relationships on hold for a while to concentrate on their careers.

"Well, at least your career is something *you* can control." Jemma pulled the sealed cover off the box and selected a peach-filled pastry. "How long are you staying?"

"About a week," Alana said. "Mom wants me to start the ball rolling and pack up a few things, but I'm having difficulty motivating myself. The house is so full of memories, it's almost overwhelming. How did you know I was here?"

"A lucky guess. I saw a fancy car pull into Essie's driveway last night." Jemma laughed. "When it was still there this morning, I figured it was you." She glanced at Alana's Mercedes. "You're the only one I know who can afford wheels like that."

Alana selected one of the puffy little pastries and tasted it. Hmmm.... This one had almond filling, her favorite. "I traded in my old car last spring and bought the Mercedes. You didn't see it at the funeral because I rode with my parents."

At the mention of Essie's burial, a moment of uncomfortable silence fell upon their conversation.

"I feel so bad about what happened to Essie." Jemma's voice grew thick as her eyes filled with tears. "I still can't believe it. One day I'm cutting flowers in her garden and chatting with her about taking her next cruise and a day later I'm in the backyard, kneeling on the sidewalk by her lifeless body—"

Alana cleared her throat and clutched her coffee mug with both hands. "I'm sorry you had to be the one to find her. It must have been traumatic."

"It was the worst shock I've ever had in my life..." Jemma said, her voice trailing off in a whisper. She picked up a napkin and dabbed her eyes. "Reid was there, too. He heard me screaming and literally vaulted over the fence to see what was wrong."

"Reid? Who is that?"

"Don't you remember him?" Jemma pointed to the large, two-story house next door with white siding and black trim. "Essie's neighbor, Reid Sinclair. He moved in last fall. He was at the funeral."

Alana stared at the man's house and the huge oak trees towering over it, feeling guilty that she hadn't had the time since last fall to come back to Merrick for a visit. "I'm sorry, I guess I was too preoccupied at the time to notice. Is that the man who had Grandma Essie caring for his daughter when he went out of town?"

"Yeah." Jemma picked up her mug and blew on her steaming coffee. "He doesn't believe Essie tripped on the stairs. He checked out the back porch and said the treads were both level and firm. She always used the handrail."

What? How would he know this? Alana froze. "Why would he think that?"

With brows raised, Jemma glanced around, as though making sure no one could overhear them. "According to Reid, she hit her head too hard for simply falling down the stairs," Jemma declared in a low-pitched voice. "He said it looked to him like someone had pushed her." She let out a long sigh. "There was so much blood…"

Alana didn't know if any of the neighbors were within hearing distance, but to ensure the conversation stayed private, she leaned close. "The house hadn't been burglarized. In fact, nothing had been disturbed so that's why the police ruled it an accident. Why didn't he speak up if he felt so strongly about her being the victim foul play?"

"He did!" Jemma's eyes flashed with indignation. "Jim Newman was the first cop to respond to Reid's call. Jim disagreed with Reid's opinion and the other officers who showed up supported Jim's assessment." Her mouth tightened with anger. "Reid had a fit when they stood by their decision, but no one would listen to him."

"I'd like to speak to your friend about that."

"I'll introduce you." Jemma's sadness lifted as her eyes softened. "He and I are dating…"

"Oh, really?" Alana smiled and refilled her coffee, relieved that the subject had steered toward something more pleasant. "Is it serious?"

"We've only had one date so far," Jemma said with a shrug, "but we talk nearly every day."

"Sounds promising. You and he must have a lot in common."

"His daughter, Hannah, is in my kindergarten class this year," Jemma continued as she reached into the box and chose an apricot-filled kolache. "He's a single parent, so he's working through the registration process by himself."

Alana washed down her pastry with sips of hot coffee. "Am I being too nosy if I ask what happened to the child's mother?"

"I don't know much about it," Jemma replied seriously, "because he's pretty tight-lipped when it comes to her, but the gossip around town is that his ex-wife gave him full custody in the divorce." She lifted her hand and gestured toward the house, her beaded bangle bracelets jingling against her arm. "Reid is self-employed and he works out of his home office, so he depended upon Essie to take Hannah when he had a pressing deadline or when he went out of town." She wiped her fingers on her napkin. "Essie told me she was the only one he trusted."

"No kidding?" Alana curiously glanced toward Reid Sinclair's house. "I wonder what that's all about."

Before Jemma could reply, a mid-sized dog with a long, shaggy coat, stopped at the open gate and timidly peered up at them. The moment Alana made eye contact with the smoky gray animal it began to whimper. She glanced at Jemma. "Is that your dog?"

Jemma shook her head. "I think it's a stray. I've seen it wandering around town for a couple weeks. I'm surprised Animal Control hasn't

22

picked it up yet."

"Poor thing. Look how thin and bony it is. It must be hungry." Alana broke off a piece of her pastry and tossed it to the animal. The dog cautiously walked up the sidewalk, sniffed the offered morsel and proceeded to wolf it down. "Gosh, that dog *is* hungry." She rose from the table. "I have to find something to feed it."

"I don't think you should do that," Jemma argued. "I know you have a big heart, Alana, but it'll never leave if you do."

Alana opened the screen door and looked back at the pitiful canine resting on the sidewalk. "Well, I can't just let it starve. I have to do something."

She went into the kitchen, grabbed a few pieces of cheese and lunchmeat and filled a small bowl with fresh water. By the time she returned to the porch, the dog was waiting on the steps. "Here you go, Dusty," she said and knelt to set everything on the step. The dog gobbled the food and drank most of the water.

"Dusty?" Jemma laughed. "Are you already giving it a name?"

"I need to call it something other than simply *dog*. That seems so demeaning to me." She petted the pooch. A smudge of oily dirt stuck to her palm. This dog desperately needed a bath. "What type of breed do you think it is?"

Jemma turned in her chair and studied the animal. "A mix of some sort. It's obviously part German shepherd. And maybe some black lab? Oh, and it's a *she*. I'm no expert myself, but I'd say the dog is still a pup—maybe six to eight months old."

Alana bent down and petted Dusty again. "How sad for it to be homeless at such a young age." She rose and went into house to wash her hands.

When she returned, Jemma drained her coffee and stood. "I have to get some craft supplies today for my new class so I need to get going, but I'll stop by later if I get the chance." A slight breeze fluffed her long coppery ropes of spiral curls. "We should meet at the bar uptown for happy hour before you go back to Minneapolis. I'll tell you all about Reid."

Alana nodded enthusiastically. "Yes, that would be great! How about happy hour *and* dinner?"

"It's a date!" Jemma bounded down the steps, her long skirt swirling. "I'll call you!"

"Okay! Bye!" Alana watched her oldest friend walk away, replaying Jemma's words in her mind.

He doesn't believe Essie tripped on the stairs…

Why? The very thought of someone deliberately pushing Grandma Essie to her death sent shivers down Alana's spine.

Though it was only one man's opinion, she needed to ask Reid Sinclair about it—soon.

***

The rest of the day unfolded in blessed peace and quiet. As Jemma predicted, the dog curled up by the front door on the porch and never left.

Toward late afternoon, Alana grabbed one of Grandma Essie's vinyl shopping bags and took the footpath behind the house to the grocery store. The path ran parallel to the back boundaries of all the houses on the block and wound through a small copse of trees, down the hill to the center of town. It ended at the public parking lot which was situated at the north end of Main Street.

Alana stopped into the grocery store for dog food then treated herself to a soft-serve cone dipped in chocolate. The afternoon temperature had reached eighty degrees and as the sun waned, the air began to cool, creating a pleasant evening.

She hiked back up the hill, her bag now heavy with five pounds of dry dog food and assorted cans of wet food. Due to yesterday's early rain, she had to step carefully along the wet, slippery earth, making sure to watch out for loose rocks or exposed tree roots. The last thing she needed was to trip and fall, scraping her knees and ruining her dress.

As she neared the top of the hill, she heard a man's deep, angry voice. It sounded like it came from the backyard next door. Without warning, a large furry animal—soaking wet—streaked across the path, disappearing into the brush. Horrified, she gasped. That looked like Dusty! What had happened to her?

"What on earth is going on?" she said aloud.

The shopping bag landed with a loud thud as she let it drop to the ground. She slammed her purse on the flat stump of a sawed-off tree. With a surge of anger spurring her on, Alana charged along the path, her arms swinging as she searched for the person responsible for spraying water at Dusty and frightening her. She couldn't permanently keep Dusty, but even so, the poor thing had taken up residence on her porch and for now, that gave her a sense of responsibility toward the sweet canine.

It didn't take her long to find the culprit. Just beyond the thick stand of lilac bushes that had initially shielded her view, a man stood at the edge of the adjacent property with his back to her, watering a young apple tree with a garden hose. This must be Drew Sinclair, the man Jemma thought so highly of…

How dare he point that hose at Dusty and chase her off! Who does he think he is?

Her fists clenched with fury as she stomped toward the tall, lean man with thick blond hair, clad in a pair of snug-fitting jeans and a black T-shirt stretched over wide, muscular shoulders. The moment she brushed past the lilacs, he suddenly spun around, showering her with icy cold water. "I told you to get—"

"What—a-a-a-ah!" Alana gasped in shock then screamed as the frigid water deluged her, saturating her from head to toe. "Stop! Turn it off!"

"Where did you—how did you…" Looking totally flummoxed by her presence, he quickly turned off the sprayer, his deep blue eyes widening as he tossed the hose away and approached her. "I'm truly sorry, I didn't mean to get you all wet! I didn't realize you were there until it was too late. When I heard the brush moving, it sounded like that coyote had come back—"

"That was no *coyote*. That was a homeless dog you were picking on!" She shivered, freezing cold by now. Clutching her skirt, she shook the water from it and glared at him, unimpressed with his convenient excuse. "Look at what you did to me! My dress is soaked, my hair is sopping wet, my shoes are probably ruined!"

"You're shivering." He reached out to warm her upper arms with his hands, but she jerked away. "You need to get warm. I'll grab a blanket for you from my porch—"

"*No thanks*. I'm going home to change." She needed a nice hot bath to warm her up and a glass of wine to calm her down. She turned to leave, then whirled around, firing one last question at him. "What did you think you were doing, attacking a poor, defenseless dog?"

"This town has been having major problems with coyotes lately. Some people have had their pets snatched right out of their yards. My daughter would be devastated if her cat disappeared." He held out his palms in frustration. "I didn't mean it any harm. I simply wanted to discourage it from coming onto my property."

"Well," she replied acidly, "I think you've gotten your wish. Neither the dog nor I will *ever* bother you again."

***

She stood before him, tall and curvy in a dripping flowered

sundress with a tiny waistline and flared skirt. Her long, dark hair, reaching just below her elbows, glistened with moisture in the late afternoon sun. Everything about her, from her manicured nails to her beautiful jewelry suggested she was a woman of fine taste. His younger self would have been attracted to her type like a magnet, but nowadays, with the pain of Monique's betrayal still deep in his heart, Reid stayed far away from classy women like her.

Just the same, he felt like a fool for turning the hose on her. He should have looked first instead of acting on impulse. Her dress and shoes were probably ruined. Judging by the incensed look on her face, so was any chance to make things right. Even so, he had to try.

"I'm sorry about your dress," he offered with sincerity. "If you'd like to drop it off at the drycleaners in town, I'll pay to have it cleaned and pressed."

"That won't be necessary. The dress is washable. It'll be fine. I can't say the same for my dog, though. She ran away looking terrified." Her wide amber eyes flashed in disbelief as she folded her arms. "What did that poor animal ever do to you? It's simply trying to survive!"

"Hey, I said I'm sorry," he said, becoming frustrated. "I didn't know it belonged to you. If you care about it so much, why don't you take better care of it? It was so skinny and scruffy-looking I thought it was a coyote."

She rolled her eyes in annoyance. "She's a stray, but I'm feeding her in the hope that her condition will improve. After the way you just traumatized her, however, I wouldn't blame the poor pooch if she never comes back!"

They were getting nowhere. In an attempt to lead the conversation into more friendly territory, he purposely softened his tone. "That's very kind of you to take responsibility for its welfare." He extended his hand. "By the way, I'm Reid Sinclair. I didn't get your name."

"I didn't give it." She ignored his gesture of neighborliness and instead kept her arms tightly folded. "I'm Alana Morgan, Essie's granddaughter. I plan to be in town only a couple days and I'd like to be able to walk outdoors without worrying about my dog getting drenched again—or me—so do me the courtesy of finding something else to use for target practice."

Target practice? You're being ridiculous. "Look, lady, I wasn't using the dog for target practice. I told you, I simply wanted to get her out of my yard—"

With a dismissive wave of her hand, she whirled around and began walking away before he'd finished talking. Her refusal to listen to reason made his temper flare. "Well, if you don't like it then from now on maybe you should keep your dog in your own yard!"

The instant the retort left his lips he regretted it. He hadn't meant to come across as a bully, and he didn't know why he'd suddenly lost his cool with her, but there was no way to take the comment back now. He stood in silence and watched her walk away, disappointed in himself for insulting Essie's granddaughter. He should have tried harder to sympathize with her reasons for being upset instead of alienating her further. She was the one person who might believe his theory that Essie had been pushed off her back steps. That Essie had been *murdered*.

She said she'd be around for merely a couple days. Given their disastrous meeting tonight, he might not get another chance to speak to her, but if he did, he had to find a way to bring up the subject and tell Alana Morgan what was on his mind.

Essie deserved that much

.

Chapter Three

The next morning, Alana stood on the back porch in a knee-length nightshirt, munching on a kolache as she endured her mother's endless questions on the phone. She didn't feel like talking, but her low mood didn't have anything to do with her mother. The real problem was that she couldn't quit thinking about her confrontation last night with Reid Sinclair and the way she'd treated him. She rarely exhibited such bad manners, but when she realized he'd frightened away Dusty by spraying the dog with water, she'd reacted without thinking, allowing her emotions to rule her heart. Her rush to judgement, however, may have ruined her chance to befriend him and ask him why he believed Grandma Essie's fall hadn't been an accident.

"Alana! Are you listening?"

"Um…yeah," Alana mumbled as she gazed across the backyard and watched an apple drop from Grandma Essie's favorite apple tree. It landed on the thick grass with a deep thump and probably had a nice bruise where it hit the ground, but it wouldn't go to waste. Several whitetail deer with their fawns in tow passed through the yard last night and had cleaned up all the fallen fruit. They probably made this spot a regular stop.

A few feet away, Dusty lay on her stomach in a relaxed posture on the floor, her full bowl of dry dog food securely between her front paws.

"Have you started going through the house?" Her mother, Terra Morgan, asked in a brisk tone, jarring Alana's thoughts.

"Somewhat," Alana answered vaguely as she leaned against a wooden pillar and popped the last bite of the kolache into her mouth. *I opened the closet door, dodged a couple things falling off the top shelf and lost my ambition...*

"So, how much progress have you made? I was hoping when you finished separating out your things and the items Grandma left you, you'd help me out by packing up all the knickknacks and glassware. We've rented a storage unit in town and it's all going in there...for now."

Grandma Essie never let go of anything. She had a cabinet filled with Fostoria crystal, china and other beautiful items from her wedding back when she was sixteen! The thought of carefully wrapping all that stuff in newspaper and arranging it in boxes made Alana shudder. This little project—a favor to her mother—was turning into a major ordeal.

"I've started filling a large plastic container." *Actually, I opened the lid and set it in the upstairs hallway. It's filled with air. Does that count?*

"Well, try to make some progress because Dad and I might be dropping by next week with a realtor to show him around the property. It would be nice if you also got some of the closets cleaned out and took all of the clothes to the thrift shop in town. Any boxes you got packed could go straight to the storage locker."

How did packing up a few things turn into a major cleaning job and hauling everything across town? Some vacation this turned out to be!

"Yeah, okay," Alana replied with a sigh. She stared across the lawn, distracted by the tall weeds choking out the perennials in Grandma Essie's flower garden.

What a shame, she thought as a wave of sadness washed over her. *Grandma Essie would never have allowed her flowers to get into such disrepair. She loved them so much. I should clean out the garden for her. That's what she'd do…*

At the same time, a little voice in her head pointed out the futility of spending all day weeding instead of getting her work done. Did she want to be slaving at this all week? Still, working in the garden held more appeal than cleaning out old coats, clothing and shoes. Besides, she needed time to get used to the idea of dismantling the most precious moments of her childhood piece by piece…

Alana pushed herself away from the pillar. "I'd better get going, Mom." She grabbed her steaming mug of coffee and took a sip. "It looks like I've got a lot to do today."

"Okay, honey. I'll call you later to see how things are coming along."

Alana hung up and turned off her phone, not in the mood for giving her mother updates on her progress. Or lack thereof.

The bright morning sun poked through the treetops as she changed into a pair of capri-length jeans and a navy, short-sleeved tunic top with a white paisley print then donned a pair of tennis shoes and swept her hair into a loose ponytail. She grabbed a few tools from Grandma's gardening shed, a plastic bucket, gloves and set them all in a small wheelbarrow. Dusty followed close on her heels.

Heavy patches of weeds dwarfed many of the perennial flowers. Until Grandma Essie's death, the garden had been tended regularly, but it hadn't taken long for the weeds to take over. A rainbow of brightly colored phlox blooms poked out between the ragweed and tall grass. Alana rolled her wheelbarrow over to the large flower bed. As she began to pull weeds, time passed quickly. She spent most of the morning cleaning up the rows of flowers, her mood brightening as the hours went by. Dusty stretched out on the soft grass and napped while she worked.

The temperature zoomed, heating up the air as a southerly breeze increased the humidity. She'd decided to quit for the day when she encountered a waist-high box elder tree growing next to a section of pink turtleheads. She grabbed the skinny tree by the trunk and tried to pull it up, but her hands slipped on the smooth, reed-like stem and she fell backwards onto the ground.

"Oh!" The word came out like a screech. Lying on her back, she brushed stray hairs from her forehead with the back of her gloved hand and looked up at the sky as Dusty rushed over to her. A hot, sticky tongue licked her face.

"Did you get a owie?"

What? Turning away from the dog, Alana lifted her head and glanced around. *Who said that?*

"Are you gonna cry now?" It sounded like the little voice came from the direction of the picket fence lining the far side of the driveway.

Alana sat up, stretched the kink out of her neck and looked toward the fence, but all she saw were tall, pink hollyhocks. Where was that little voice coming from?

"Does Grandma Essie know you're pulling out her flowers?"

Alana looked straight ahead and saw a small, cherubic face framed with curly blonde hair poking through the phlox. She blinked in surprise at her unexpected visitor and pulled off her gloves. "Grandma Essie? Um…well, I'm helping her. She…she went to heaven."

The little girl's mouth opened wide, forming a perfect O. "She *did*? Can we go there and visit her?"

"Well," Alana said patiently, "I don't think so. It's kind of far away."

The little girl shrugged. "My da-dee has a car. He can drive fast." She wagged her finger. "But he says you haf to sit still in the car seat," Her brows knitted together in total seriousness as she nodded her head. "What's your name?"

Alana focused on standing up and brushing the dirt from her clothes to keep from chuckling at the exceptional cuteness of this delightful child. "It's Alana. What's yours?"

The little girl pushed her way through the flowers. "I'm Hannah." She wore a pair of peach shorts and a matching T-shirt. Her fine blonde curls needed brushing. "Can I haf a flower?"

"Of course, you can have a whole bouquet." Alana picked a palm-sized pair of shears off the ground. "I'll cut some zinnias for you. When I was your age, Grandma Essie used to give me lots of flowers for my room." The phlox were prettier, but tended to constantly drop petals. They also played host to a variety of bugs, including small spiders. In Alana's opinion, phlox were best enjoyed in the garden or in a vase on the porch—not on the kitchen table where the spiders would drop from the petals and perhaps frighten little girls.

She began to snip off a variety of large zinnia blooms, instead, in an assortment of colors. "Where do you live, Hannah?" Alana already knew the answer but thought it would give her an excuse to bring the little girl home—and start over with her father.

"Over there." Hannah pointed toward Reid Sinclair's large white house with black trim. "My da-dee is making ha-burgers."

Before Alana had the chance to answer, Dusty rushed toward the little girl and tried to lick her hand. Hannah drew back with a frightened cry.

"It's okay," Alana said as she dropped the shears and moved close, stroking the dog's head to distract it. "Dusty won't hurt you. She likes you. See how she's wagging her tail? She wants to be friends."

Hannah stood frozen in place; her blue eyes filled with uncertainty.

Alana straightened. "Your father is probably wondering where you are about now. Let's go find him and show him your flowers." She held out the small collection. "Do you want to hold them?"

Hannah nodded and accepted the bouquet.

Alana took off her gloves and dropped them on the ground next to her shears. "I'd better confine Dusty to the porch, though. We don't want her following us into your yard. You wait here. I'll give her a treat and be right back."

Alana led the dog to the house. She grabbed a bag of meat-flavored biscuits and threw a couple toward the opposite end of the porch. Dusty ran to claim them and Alana shut the gate, securing the latch.

"Shall we go?" she asked as she walked back to the garden and found Hannah watching a small frog hop under a butterfly bush. A delicious smell wafted through the air and it seemed to be coming from the direction of the Sinclair house. The aroma of beef on the grill filled Alana's nostrils, making her stomach growl and reminding her that she hadn't eaten since breakfast.

They'd reached the driveway dividing their properties when Alana saw Reid standing at the grill with his back to her wielding a long-handled spatula. His wide, muscular shoulders flexed under his maroon T-shirt as he flipped a row of sizzling burgers. His tight jeans rode low on his hips. His wide-legged stance and straight posture exuded an air of confidence she found intriguing.

He must have sensed their presence because he turned just as she ushered Hannah through the gate and entered his yard. The moment their gazes met his deep blue eyes widened with a flicker of curiosity, but before she could react, he frowned. The wariness overshadowing his attitude communicated a distinct message—first impressions *do* count. Their heated exchange last night had obviously soured him on putting forth any effort to become friendly with her now. Consequently, striking up a conversation with him about how Essie died seemed definitely out of the question.

***

Reid wished last night had never happened, but it did and he'd ended up making things worse by losing his temper. He wanted to ignore the fact that he'd shouted at her to keep her dog out of his yard, but it was probably the main blunder in their confrontation that had upset her the most.

Alana held Hannah's hand as she escorted the little girl through the gate. He took care to search out Alana's response as they ambled toward him. The neutral expression in her beautiful eyes bore no hint of either anticipation or displeasure over having to deal with him again. She was merely going through the motions of returning an errant child. Nothing more.

"Hi, Da-dee!" Hannah smiled and held up a cluster of brightly-colored cut flowers. Some were already bent from her little fingers clutching the stems too tight. "Look what Lana gave me!"

"Very pretty. Did you thank her?"

Hannah looked up in youthful adoration at her companion. "Thank you."

Alana gazed down and smiled affectionately. "You're welcome, sweetie."

Reid approached them, the grilling spatula still in his hand. "Thank you for bringing her home."

"It was no trouble." Her breathy voice projected a soft tone, but held no emotion. "She's a darling little girl. I didn't want her to wander away from home and get lost."

The inference was clear. If he'd put as much energy into keeping track of Hannah as he did with cooking burgers, she wouldn't have had to step in…

"Thank you for your concern," he said to Alana, "and I'm sorry to inconvenience you. I'll make *sure* it doesn't happen again."

He winced inwardly. His jaw clenched. *Did I just stick my foot in my mouth a second time? Why do I keep acting like an idiot in front of Essie's granddaughter?*

"It's no problem. I'll be around for a few more days. She can come over and visit any time she likes. That is, if it's all right with you."

At first, he didn't know if she meant that as a jab at his lousy parenting or if she was using it as a bridge to leave behind yesterday's disastrous confrontation and start over on a new footing. Before he had a chance to figure out a response, Alana let go of Hannah's hand and waved goodbye as she began to step backward toward the gate. "I need to get back to work, so…" She turned and headed back to her own yard.

Hannah waved her flowers. "Bye, Lana!"

He suddenly realized his error. Pausing too long had given her the wrong impression. "Wait!" Reid held up the spatula, knowing he sounded as desperate as he probably looked. "Before you go, there's something I'd like to say. Please allow me to apologize for last night."

She halted and looked back, clearly surprised.

Encouraged by her reaction, he kept going. "I was wrong," he blurted. "I shouldn't have upset you like that, or your dog. When you confronted me, I should have let it go instead of laying the blame on you. The truth is, I would never have treated Essie that way, and I shouldn't have talked that way to you, either. I'd like us to start over."

She turned around and began to slowly walk toward him. "It's not all your fault. When you said you thought you were chasing a coyote from your yard, I shouldn't have accused you of being heartless or inconsiderate." She shrugged. "I guess we were both wrong."

He held out his hand. "Truce?"

"Okay…"

Her amber eyes twinkled as she accepted the handshake, but the moment their fingers entwined, a strong current jumped from her palm to his, stunning him. He dropped her hand and cleared his throat, even though he couldn't pull his gaze from hers. "I'd better get back to cooking before everything burns," he said, backing toward the grill. A sudden thought crossed his mind. "Why don't you stay for dinner? It would be nice to have someone besides a five-year-old to talk to for a change."

She shook her head, frowning. "I wouldn't want you to go to any trouble for me. I should get back to the garden anyway—"

"It's no trouble." He grinned. "I've got enough food to invite the entire neighborhood. C'mon. I insist. Besides, there's something I'd like to talk to you about concerning Essie."

She stared at him unblinking, as though she already suspected what he had to say and wanted to hear it. "All right. Sure." She wiped her hands on the sides of her jeans. "Just give me a moment to clean up."

"Go through the kitchen and take a right—"

"I know where it is," Alana said with a laugh. "I've been in this house more times than I can count. Growing up, I spent a lot of rainy days playing with the kids who used to live here."

"Hannah," Reid said as he walked back to the grill, "go with Alana, honey, and wash your hands."

Hannah danced her way toward the house, chattering up a storm to their dinner guest.

Reid pulled the burgers off the grill and arranged them in

hamburger buns on a platter. He was setting the table inside his three-season porch when Alana and Hannah reappeared.

Alana approached the table. "What can I do to help?"

Reid pointed toward a refrigerator along the back wall. "Help yourself to a soda and while you're at it, grab the ketchup and mustard. Oh, and get the dill slices, too, if you like pickles on your burger."

She glanced around. "I really like what you've done with this porch, adding the windows and turning it into a three-season, all-purpose room."

"Thanks. I like to sit out here in the fresh air and relax watching baseball games on TV."

He reached into a small cabinet and pulled out a stack of heavy paper plates. "Whenever I grill, we eat out here, picnic-style. I've got everything stored in this cabinet so there's no work to it at all." He set a stack of plates on the table and a silverware caddy with plastic utensils and napkins alongside it.

"I get a juice box!" Hannah raced toward the refrigerator. "I wanna help, too!"

Alana returned to the table with the condiments then arranged three place settings.

"I hope you like potato salad," Reid said as he set a gallon-sized plastic pail on the table. "I can't get enough of this stuff. I get it at the grocery store in town. The people in the deli say it's made exclusively by an elderly lady." He pulled the cover off and stuck a large spoon in it.

"Oh, that's Mrs. Wagner! She's won a lot of awards for her cooking. Nearly every kid in Merrick has grown up eating her potato salad, including me."

Loud snaps and the soft popping sound of fizzing bubbles filled the room as Reid and Alana opened their soda cans. They sat down to dinner and began to talk, but the conversation steered in a different direction than Reid had intended.

"I had breakfast with Jemma this morning," Alana said casually as she munched on potato salad. "She said you two were seeing each other and she seemed pretty happy about it."

The hand holding Reid's burger stopped in mid-air at the mention of Jemma's name. His concern grew at hearing Jemma refer to him and her as being a couple. They were friends—nothing more. "We've only had one date, if you can call it that. We had dinner together at a fundraiser about three weeks ago."

Alana gave him an embarrassed look as though she'd offended him. "Did I say something wrong? I apologize if I've raised a subject that's none of my business."

"No, it's not you." He set down his burger. "It's me. Jemma's a terrific person and I consider her a friend, but..."

"...but what?" Alana frowned; her eyes were shadowed with concern. "I hope you're not leading her on. She's been one of my best friends since we were kids and I don't want her heart to be broken over someone who isn't taking her seriously."

"Believe me, that has never been my intention."

"Then what's the problem?"

"I don't mean to sound cavalier, but she's taking our friendship too serious." Deciding to speak his mind, Reid slid his hand across the back of his neck to massage the tension in his muscles. "I met her one night while we were both standing in line at a fundraising dinner. The restaurant was full and neither of us had reservations, so when a table suddenly became available for two, I asked her if she'd like to join me. We had a great time that night and I enjoyed her company." He shrugged. "It was an impromptu evening between two strangers, but she took it to be more than that. She calls me every day."

"Then ask her to stop."

"I have," Reid argued. "She always makes some excuse for why she needs a minute of my time. An hour later, I'm still trying to end the conversation and get back to work. I usually let all my calls go to voicemail, but Hannah currently has an obsession with answering the phone and waits for Jemma to call every day." He let out a frustrated sigh. "Look, she's Hannah's kindergarten teacher. I need to handle this delicately, but so far, I haven't been able to figure out a way to get through to her without hurting her feelings."

"Maybe *you're* getting the wrong idea," Alana argued with a hint of annoyance in her voice. "Maybe she just wants someone to talk to who has more going on in their life than adjusting to their first year of school. She's intelligent, fun-loving and has a terrific sense of humor. If a woman like Jemma doesn't appeal to you, who would?"

A woman like you…but I've been down that road once before and don't care to repeat the same mistake again.

"At this point in my life," he said quietly, "my daughter and my business are my chief concerns."

He snatched his burger off his plate and took a huge bite. Better to have his mouth full than to talk about his past. In the two encounters he'd had with Alana, he already knew she and Monique not only shared the same tastes in just about everything, but both were also independent and strong-willed. He doubted, however, that Alana would ever pull the narcissistic stunt on him and Hannah that Monique had. Even so, his failed marriage had made him cautious of all women now. Hannah was too important to him to risk subjecting her to another bad relationship.

After dinner, Hannah went to her room to get her favorite stuffed animal, a lion, to show Alana. Reid and Alana began clearing the table. "Now that Hannah's out of earshot," he said earnestly, "I'd like to talk to you about Essie." He snapped the cover back on the pail of potato salad and looked up, meeting Alana's questioning gaze. "I know this is going to sound far-fetched, and some of the details may be upsetting, but please hear me out."

"Jemma mentioned you had a different idea about what happened to Grandma Essie than what the local police have officially ruled." She stood back and clasped her hands. "Go ahead, but never mind soft-pedaling the situation. I want to hear what *you* think. All of it."

He stopped what he was doing and leaned his hands on the table, facing her. "I've carefully scrutinized every inch of the back steps of Essie's house. They're in perfect condition. In other words, I don't think she fell by accident. I honestly don't see how she could. She paid attention to her surroundings and always gripped the railing with her right hand. I saw her do it, time and time again. I believe someone— most likely a man—pushed her." He steeled himself as Alana's face paled. "She hit the sidewalk with much stronger force than if she'd merely fainted or tripped. Hard enough to cause the extreme head injury that she had incurred." Knowing someone was getting away with her murder made his anger flare. "I don't know who is responsible, or why, but I feel I owe it to her to find out."

Alana's cheeks flushed as her eyes pooled with tears. "Why would someone want to harm her? The police found no evidence of a break-in or robbery. What would be the attacker's motive?"

"I don't know." He straightened, jamming his hands into his jean pockets. "That question keeps eating at me. Maybe the intruder was interrupted, or maybe he *did* get what he was after and no one has discovered it yet." He stared out the window, gazing at Essie's house. "Just before she died, Essie told me she was tired of people trying to take advantage of her because she was elderly. At the time, I assumed she was talking about a telemarketer, but now I'm not so sure that's what she meant. Given the circumstances, I don't think it should be ruled it out."

"Have you spoken to the police about this?"

"You bet I did." He snorted. "Instead of getting their cooperation, I got laughed at. The cops told me to go home and mind my own business. Stop playing amateur detective."

"I can understand why. This town has always been quiet and very peaceful," Alana said as she gathered the plates and napkins. "When I was a kid, no one ever locked their homes and most people left the keys in their cars." As she stared into his eyes, her beautiful face filled with worry. "What are you going to do now?"

He picked up his empty cola can and crushed it with his fingers. "What can I do? No one believes me."

"I do," she replied stubbornly. "Investigate her death yourself."

"What makes you think I'm qualified to investigate a murder?"

She frowned. "If you don't, who will?"

Her enthusiasm surprised him. "You're right about that, but I'm not sure where to start." The answer suddenly seemed clear. "I've got an idea. How about we team up together?"

She blinked with astonishment, clearly taken aback at his suggestion. "I only have a week and that's not nearly enough time to launch an investigation. Besides, I'm supposed to be cleaning out closets and packing knickknacks and china." She sighed. "I'm sorry," she said, sounding regretful. "The offer is tempting, but I can't do both. My parents would have a fit if they found out I'd spent the time investigating a hunch. My dad would scoff at it and say I was 'chasing my tail.' They believe unequivocally what the police told them."

With the deadline looming for the final draft of his speech and the outline of his next book due soon after that, he didn't have a minute to spare either. If anything, he should be working around the clock to catch up, but he'd been struggling with the circumstances surrounding Essie's death for a month and the nagging questions in the back of his mind weren't going to go away until he'd satisfied his curiosity beyond a shadow of a doubt.

"You're right," he said seriously. "I'm supposed to be finalizing a speech and that's just the tip of the iceberg. My schedule is relentless, but this is too important to let slide." He let out a deep breath. "Somehow, some way, I've got to do this."

Chapter Four

On Monday morning, Alana sat on the front porch with her pink bathrobe wrapped tightly around her, drinking coffee and munching on the last Kolache when her phone beeped. Not in the mood to talk yet, she carelessly glanced at it. The text came from her superior, Chad Thompson, the product director of her team at work.

"R U in town?"

Curious, she texted him back. *"No, in Merrick. Why?"*

"Something's going on at the office."

She sighed, irritated that she couldn't even take two weeks off without dealing with work issues.

"What now? Call me…"

She drummed her fingers on the table. "When I finish my coffee," she murmured to herself and pushed the phone away, fuming over being dragged into some issue that her team could—no, *should*—be able to solve while she was on vacation.

Two minutes later, the phone rang.

Rolling her eyes, she hit the answer button and put it on

speakerphone. "Hi, Chad. What's the problem?"

"I don't know," he blurted. "I just don't know."

She froze at the panic in his voice. Chad never lost his cool over anything, so for something to get him this emotional, it had to be critical. Her feet slipped off the chair next to her and she sat up straight, her senses on full alert. "What's happening? Did you get a bomb scare in the building or something?"

"No, it's much worse than that. I got to the office this morning at my usual time, seven sharp and found all the lights off. The place was deserted." He let out a tense breath. "And the doors were locked."

"What?" She jumped out of her chair. "Was there any communication posted on the door? Any email in your inbox explaining why?"

"No, and that's what worries me most. I can't access my email. It looks like the company has simply shut down."

She swallowed hard, reluctant to accept his conclusion. That would mean hundreds of dedicated employees were left stranded with no explanation. "Are you certain?"

"Well, it's eight-thirty and the office is still as dark as a tomb. I just checked. What else am I supposed to think?"

"Okaay…" Alana thought for a moment. "What's coming down the grapevine?"

"Confusion." The roar of traffic echoed in the background, indicating he was walking somewhere outdoors, probably along Nicollet Mall, the heart of the retail district in downtown Minneapolis. "Everyone is asking the same questions, but no one is getting any answers. The team is gathering at the coffeeshop in the IDS courtyard at ten this morning to talk about the situation." Traffic sounds ceased, giving way to soft music. He must have left the street and entered a building. "I've got three kids to feed, two car payments and a big mortgage. If this is the end of my job, I don't know what I'm going to do…"

She didn't know what to say to reassure him. Nervous, she picked up her phone and walked into the house. "I'm about an hour away, but I still need time to park and hoof it over to the IDS Center." The wooden screen door slammed behind her. "As soon as I hang up, I'll jump into the shower and get there as close to ten as I can."

"Great. See you there but don't speed. I don't want you getting a ticket."

Leave it to Chad to worry about something like that at a time like *this*.

She hurried upstairs to shower and change into a pair of denim leggings and a blue and white print top with pintucks and three-quarter sleeves with ruffled cuffs. She slipped on a pair of flats, grabbed her purse and dashed out of the house. She'd planned to meet with Reid today to go over his plan to gather evidence on Grandma Essie's fall, but that would have to wait. Finding out the status of her job took priority.

She set a dish of wet food for Dusty on the back porch and jumped into her car. The weather was good and traffic was fairly light on Interstate 35, so the trip took her a little over an hour. Once downtown, she pulled into the underground parking facility under the Dorale office building and tried her security card. It worked! She parked her car in the nearly-empty garage and took the stairs to the street level. The only vehicles there were in the spaces reserved for building security personnel and custodians.

By the time she reached the IDS Center her fitness tracker read ten-fifteen. Her team had pushed several tables together in the center courtyard. Alana bought a large cup of coffee and a vanilla cream breakfast scone at the coffeeshop and approached them. Everyone greeted her with tentative smiles. Chad Thompson had saved a chair for her next to his.

She set her purse and coffee cup on the table and turned to Chad, a heavyset middle-aged man wearing khaki slacks and a light blue striped summer shirt. "What's the latest news?"

Chad ran his hand through his short reddish hair. "Nothing yet. Not a blasted thing. My wife keeps texting me to find out if I've heard anything." He let out a deep, frustrated sigh. "I hope we're not all going to be standing in the unemployment line tomorrow but it sure looks that way."

The dozen members of her team began to grumble. Where were technical leads and developers going to find jobs in a down-turned market where very little was available? A female coworker, one of the technical leads, had a Target-brand box of tissues setting on the table in front of her. She pulled one out and began to dab at her eyes.

Alana let out a worried sigh. *Never mind that promotion I wanted to go after. I need to find out if I still have a job...*

"Gee," Alana said in a worried tone. "I'm thirty-two and I've never applied for unemployment in my life. Where would I go to get it? Is the line long?"

"Nah." Chad leaned his large body back in his chair and smiled at her naivete. "Actually, it's all done online now."

Alana reached into her purse and pulled out the flat paper bag containing her scone. "Well, at least I'll be able to pay my bills."

Chad gave a wry chortle. "On $740 a week? That's the maximum they pay in Minnesota, you know. Good luck!"

Alana set the bag on the table, leaving the scone inside. She'd suddenly lost her appetite. She'd always made good money in her field and as a product manager for Dorale Software Solutions, her current salary was in the six-figure range. She didn't have kids to feed, but she did have some hefty student loans for her master's degree from St.

Thomas University, a mortgage and a car payment. Chad was right. Unemployment wouldn't begin to cover it.

I'll just have to get my resume polished up, upload it to all the employment search engines and hit the ground running looking for another position. I've never had a problem with finding a good job in my life. The job market is tight right now, but with a little luck, I won't need to be on unemployment long.

At noon, with no word from the company, the group disbanded. Some went straight to the bar to continue commiserating over their dire situation. Others went home. Everyone acknowledged the next step was to update their resumes and start looking for new jobs.

Alana said her goodbyes with hugs and promised she'd keep in touch. She called her mother to give her parents the grim news as she walked back to the Dorale building to retrieve her car. Once she arrived, she ended the call but instead of taking the stairs to the lower parking level, she tried the front door on the street level. To her surprise, the glass double-doors whispered opened. Her footfalls echoed on the granite floor through the deserted, two-story lobby as she walked toward the elevators. At the elevator bank, she swiped her card, pressed the button for the tenth floor and stood back as it whisked her upward. She wanted to see the place for herself.

At the tenth floor, the doors opened. She stepped one foot off the elevator and peered to her left, staring through the glass walls dividing the elevator bank from the reception area. Chad had described it perfectly. The office appeared as dark and dead as a tomb. With a disappointed sigh, she backed into the elevator and went down to retrieve her car.

She drove to her condo at the southern edge of downtown. She needed to check on the place, collect her mail and take a quiet break before heading back to Merrick. On her way, she encountered several stoplights—not an unusual occurrence when driving downtown. She happened to catch a red light a block from Marquette Towers. As she pulled up to the crosswalk and waited a familiar thunderous laugh caught her attention. An Irish tavern with an outdoor patio was situated on the corner next to her car. She glanced to her right and did a double take. Dylan O'Rourke, her sandy-haired, blue-eyed, smooth-talking ex-fiancé sat leisurely at a table under a bright green umbrella with his arm around a curvy blonde.

The woman looked familiar—even *with* all her clothes on. The scene of that day when she'd caught them in the shower flashed through her mind, piercing her with fresh anger. "You were *so* desperate to get me back," she murmured. "Falling all over yourself with contrition. Promising to never see her again." She uttered a bitter laugh. "You two deserve each other."

The car behind her honked, letting her know the light had changed. She looked straight ahead and gunned the gas pedal, anxious to leave before Dylan saw her. She sped away and never looked back. Driving back to Merrick for the rest of the week to get a break from all her issues held more appeal now than ever.

On the next block, she pulled into Marquette Towers, parked in her reserved spot, retrieved her mail and took the elevator to her condo. As she unlocked the door and walked inside, she looked around and wondered how she was going to pay for this place now.

"I should have spent less on my lifestyle and put more money aside," she whispered to herself. The money she'd expended on decorating this place with almond-colored leather furniture, fine arts and a six-foot, flat screen Sony TV would have paid the mortgage for a year. As it was, she only had enough money in her checkbook to cover one month's bills.

Still in the entryway, she tossed her mail on the console table. She paid all her bills electronically so her snail mail consisted of mostly junk items. One envelope slid away from the stack. A white business-sized envelope with a return address from Doral Software Systems. She snatched it and ripped it open, staring with dismay at the words on the page. Doral had officially closed its doors. It existed no more as of last Friday. Worse yet, she'd get her last pay check at the end of the month, but her health care coverage would end at that time and severance pay would not be forthcoming...

She needed to get another job—and fast.

***

Reid stood on Essie's back porch and knocked on the door. As if she'd been standing in the kitchen, waiting for him, Alana jerked open the heavy wooden door, swinging it wide. The aroma of freshly-brewed coffee wafted through the opening. "Hello, Reid—"

"I need to talk to you," he broke in as his gaze swept over her, distracting him. "I...ah..." She looked terrific in denim leggings and that form-fitting blue top. Her long, dark hair fell like thick strands of silk to her elbows. "I know it's late and last minute, too, but if we hurry, we still have time. I'd planned to come over this morning, but my agent called early and needed me to make some changes to the outline of my next book. I had to take care of that first, and I didn't realize how much time it took or I would have called you." It wasn't like him to be so forgetful. "Nate, my agent, he's kind of a stickler for details. Well, the guy's obsessive-compulsive, if you ask me, but I guess that's what makes him so good at his job."

She sighed and gestured with her hand, beckoning him to come in. "Well, at least he *has* a job."

Instead of entering Essie's large, old-fashioned kitchen, he stopped at the doorframe, confused. "What do you mean by that?"

"I got a call early this morning myself. My employer went out of business at eleven fifty-nine PM last Friday. When my director showed up for work today, he found the place locked up tight. I had to make a run to the Twin Cities for an emergency meeting with my coworkers. I just got back."

"I'm sorry to hear that." Reid shoved his hands into his pockets, his usual response when he didn't know what else to do. "What are your plans now?"

"Well, I guess I'll apply for unemployment," she said wearily, "and start looking for another job." She stepped aside. "Aren't you going to come in?"

"Actually, the reason I dropped by was to ask if you would go uptown with me." He checked his watch. "If we hurry, we can make it to the police station before the shift change."

"To do what?" She frowned. "Get a copy of the police report?"

"That, too," he said, taking a step forward. "You need to speak with the cop who was on duty the day Essie was found so you can ask him some questions."

"Like…what type of questions?"

"Like the same ones *I* asked him, but didn't get any decent answers for my trouble. And anything else that comes up at the time."

She considered the idea for a moment. "Okay. That makes sense." She shut off the coffeemaker and reached for her purse, a sardonic grin curling the corners of her mouth. "So, you think if I smile coyly and bat my eyelashes at him, I'll get more out of him than you did?"

"Of course not." He responded with a wry laugh. "I wouldn't ask you to approach him like that. He might cooperate with you, though, if you come at it from the angle that you're looking for more information because you're Essie's granddaughter."

"That's a good point," Alana said, pulling the house keys from her purse. "By the way, where's Hannah?"

"She's with Jemma until five o'clock. I asked Jemma to take care of her today because I had a tight timeframe to get something back to my agent."

Alana glanced at the kitchen clock. "That doesn't give us a lot of time, but it's doable."

He stepped onto the back porch waiting as Alana locked the back door. "Do you mind if we walk? We'll take the path down to the center of town."

"Not at all. It's a great shortcut and doesn't take any longer than driving." She slipped her keys into her purse and slung the strap over her shoulder. "I like to walk and I could use the fresh air. Besides, it'll give us a chance to talk about the situation before we get there."

They walked along the back sidewalk to the garage then took the sloping path down to the public parking lot located along the edge of the business district. Across the lot, the city maintenance garage, a small cinderblock building, sat next to the police station. A black and white cruiser pulled up in front of the building as they were crossing the street. They stood at the curb until the officer parked and got out of the vehicle before they approached him.

Officer Strand wore a tan shirt with dark brown pocket flaps and epaulets and dark brown slacks. The flap on his right breast pocket had *B. Strand* stitched in white. Above that was a patch of the American flag. His badge, a silver metal star, was pinned above his left pocket. His reddish-blond hair had been buzzed close to his scalp.

His attention zeroed in on Alana. "May I help you?"

"Hello," she said with a note of confidence in her voice. "I'm Alana Morgan, Essie Anderson's granddaughter."

"My condolences, Ms. Morgan, on the loss of your grandmother."

"Thank you. I'd like to ask you some questions about her death and where she was discovered." She and Reid gone over the list of things for her to ask on the walk to the station.

Officer Strand's face showed no emotion, but the way he gripped his hands on his duty gear belt suggested to Reid he didn't want to be grilled about it. "It's all covered in my narrative in the incident report. I suggest you go inside and see my administrative assistant. She'll order a copy for you."

"Thank you," Alana said in a soft, feminine voice. "I'll do that, but I do have a few questions for you in the meantime."

The lines around Sheriff Strand's mouth tightened. His brown eyes stared at her with intensity.

"From what my mother tells me, Grandma Essie was found with her face to one side on the sidewalk in a pool of blood and her glasses had been thrown from her head. The palms of her hands were badly scraped and one of her wrists was broken as well. Besides her head injury, the issue with her hands suggests to me she hit the ground quite hard."

"Most older women are frail," Sheriff Strand replied with a tone of finality in his voice. "If she fell from the top step, she would have hit the sidewalk fairly hard."

"Or, if someone pushed her…"

"*If* someone pushed her." Sheriff Strand shook his head. "We found no evidence of a break in and your mother verified nothing was taken from the home or appeared to be out of place. As far as we know, Mrs. Anderson didn't have any enemies, so there was no motive for anyone to take her life."

"But it's possible…"

"Anything is possible, Ms. Morgan, but there needs to be evidence."

"Perhaps she knew her attacker," Alana quickly countered, "and either let the person into the house or went out on the back porch to speak to them."

"*If* she was attacked. As I said, there is no evidence to support that theory."

Reid stepped forward. "What about the porch light? From what I understand, she'd been lying there since the evening before. If she'd left the house on her own terms, she would have surely turned on the light."

Sheriff Strand responded with an annoyed shrug. "Perhaps it wasn't completely dark out so she didn't see the need to put on the light."

A call came over the Sheriff's radio. He answered it using his lapel mic then said, "I have to go."

"Just one more thing," Reid persisted as he followed the officer to his car. "Essie always wore a medical alert device around her neck but it was missing when her body was delivered to the funeral home. What happened to it?"

The sheriff opened his car door. "I don't know anything about that," he said with a dismissive wave of his hand. "I didn't see any device on her. Get the report. Have a good day."

He jumped into his car, turned on his rooftop lightbar and siren and sped away.

Reid stood next to Alana, watching the squad car disappear around the corner. "Well, that wasn't as bad as the last time I talked to him, but still not very productive. What do you think? Do you want me to keep pursuing this inquiry?"

Alana turned toward the police station and let out a wry chuckle. "More than ever. His answers raised more questions than I had before talking to him. Let's go and order that report."

They took care of business then turned toward home. At the narrow footpath, Reid stepped aside and allowed Alana to go first. They had only gone a few feet up the incline when they encountered a muddy spot.

"Careful! It's slippery here." Reid warned, but as the words were leaving his lips, Alana skidded on the soft ground.

"Ah!"

Instinctively, he reached out and caught her, his hands spanning the narrow width of her waist as his fingers pressed into the softness of her slender frame. She stood so close the sweet fragrance of her perfume wafted into his nostrils, distracting him. When she glanced over her shoulder to acknowledge his help, their gazes met. His pulse jumped. He wanted to pull her closer and bury his face in the crown of her soft hair. A little closer still and he could even kiss her…

Alana cleared her throat and straightened.

The moment passed. Reid let go of Alana and continued on, but his thoughts churned over how easily he'd allowed her attractiveness to distract him.

Stick to the investigation, Sinclair. You already have enough on your plate. Don't complicate things any more than they already are.

Jamming his hands in his pockets, he walked Alana back home in silence.

Chapter Five

Loud, familiar voices echoed through the house, waking Alana early the next morning. Sitting up in bed, she rubbed her eyes, trying to focus as she listened to the people walking through the main floor of the house. The sharp, high-pitched voice belonged to her mother. Still half asleep, Alana squinted at the clock. The glowing orange numerals read 8 am.

What are my parents doing here at this ungodly hour? Who is with them?

After such a stressful day yesterday, she'd planned to sleep in this morning and the unexpected intrusion made her grumpy. With a groan, she collapsed back on the bed and slung her arm over her eyes. So much for a quiet, *uneventful* week.

The thud of multiple footsteps coming up to the second floor invaded her cranky thoughts. It sounded like a herd of buffalo on the creaky oak stairway. "There are four bedrooms and two bathrooms up here…"

Realizing they were about to walk past her room, Alana jumped up and slid out of bed, but became disoriented and nearly fell on the floor. She managed to stumble to the bedroom door and shut it then groped her way to the closet, squinting through tired eyes for something to wear.

Terra Morgan opened the bedroom door and leaned into the room. She wore brown slacks and a green plaid tunic top. The deep, rich shine in her dark, shoulder-length bob had a reddish tinge to it. "Alana, you'd better get dressed. The realtor is here. I'm showing him the house and he needs to see this room."

The urgent tone of her mother's words irritated her, but instead of snapping back, she leaned farther into the closet. "I thought you said you were coming *next* week. I'll be ready in five minutes."

"All right. We'll view this room last. By the way, whose dog is that sleeping on the back porch and why are you feeding it?" Terra persisted.

"It's a stray, Mom." She stepped back and held up a red blouse. "I'm giving it food because it's starving."

Terra's inquisitive look turned into a disapproving frown. "Isn't that what the town animal shelter is for? Don't you think you should take it there so it can find a permanent home?"

Alana put the blouse back and pulled a yellow, V-neck top off a hanger to wear with white shorts. "I'd rather try to find a home for it myself before I leave. Then I'll know for certain it ended up in a good place."

Terra placed her hand on the door, indicating she was anxious to get back to the realtor. "Okay, but please don't allow that dog to come into the house. It probably has worms and fleas."

Alana rolled her eyes after Terra left. The dog didn't have worms and fleas, at least, not that she could tell. She stepped out of her nightgown, put on the outfit and slipped her feet into a pair of thongs. Then she quickly made the bed and left the room.

She found her parents and a short, middle-aged man standing in the master bedroom at the end of the hallway, discussing the water damage on the ceiling. "That will need to be fixed," the man said, using his pen to point at the dark stain on the ceiling and a section of the outside wall. "It looks fresh. You'll definitely need to get the roof replaced as soon as possible to avoid further deterioration."

"We've already found a dozen things to fix and now this..." Terra's face looked drawn with worry and fatigue as she stared into the eyes of her husband, Darren. "I didn't realize this house had so many issues. What are we going to do? We're flying to Miami next week. There's no way we can find a contractor and get the work done before we leave."

Alana had never seen her mother look so downcast and defeated. For nearly a year, her parents had been planning the vacation of a lifetime for their fortieth anniversary; a transatlantic cruise from Miami to Southampton, England then a tour from London to Rome. The trip would last exactly forty days.

Her tall, gray-haired father placed his hands on his hips and studied the damage. "Maybe we could put a tarp over that spot on the roof for now." After a moment, Darren turned and placed his large hands upon Terra's shoulders with a sympathetic smile. "Don't worry. We'll figure something out."

"I can help," Alana heard herself say aloud. Until now, no one had noticed her presence, but once she spoke, everyone turned to her. "Since I'm presently unemployed anyway," she said to her mother, "I can stay longer and handle some of these things for you."

Yikes! Did I really just say that? I know nothing about house repair. And as far as packing is concerned, this place has more artifacts than a museum!

If this visit had happened yesterday morning, she couldn't have volunteered to take on such a huge responsibility, but losing her job had changed everything. She had more time now than she knew what to do with, but given her financial situation, she dearly hoped her unemployed status was short-lived.

Terra's green eyes mirrored uncertainty. "Are you sure, honey? I don't want to keep you from looking for another job."

"Mom's right," Darren, chimed in. "You need to get the Sunday paper this weekend and start looking for places to apply. You've got bills to pay."

"The application process is all online now," Alana told her father seriously. "I can use the internet here in the house to search and when I get an interview, I'll just drive back home." Grandma Essie had a computer and used it mostly for email and her family genealogy research. It was old and a little slow, but it would be sufficient to surf the net. Often, the first interview took place by phone, anyway, so it didn't matter whether she was in Merrick or Minneapolis when she got the call. If the phone interview was successful in advancing her to the next phase, she'd have plenty of time to drive back to Minneapolis for a face-to-face meeting.

"The good thing is, we'd have someone to keep an eye on the place," Darren said as he put his arm around his wife. "Having Alana here would give us peace of mind so we can enjoy our trip." He pulled a money clip from his pocket and separated out a small wad of bills. "Here," he said, stuffing a couple hundred dollars into Alana's hand. "This is for gas and expenses. Buy some groceries with it, too." He held up his palm to silence Alana when she tried to protest. "You're doing Mom and me a much-needed favor and I don't want you spending your last dollar on things we should be paying for."

Terra agreed and took Alana downstairs, giving her specific instructions on what else she wanted done. "Here is the key to the storage locker we've rented in town," she said as she pulled it off her key ring." You'll need to get a stack of plastic storage containers and heavy-duty garbage bags. Pack up everything of value. The rest goes to the thrift store. Use Grandma's car. It's still insured and has a full tank of gas."

"Don't worry about anything, Mom. I'll take care of it."

Terra hugged her daughter. "You have no idea how much Dad and I appreciate this."

"What about the furniture?"

Terra hesitated. "We'll have a yard sale."

The thought of selling Grandma Essie's nice wicker furniture on the porch gave Alana a deep surge of sadness. So much of their family's memories and traditions were being dismantled and given away or sold off to total strangers. She wanted to cry, but merely nodded in agreement instead. She needed to stay strong and keep a positive attitude for her mother.

***

Later that day, Alana sat down at the large oak desk in the parlor and turned on Grandma Essie's computer to apply for unemployment and begin her search for job openings. Since her condominium resided in Minneapolis, she needed to apply for her unemployment benefit from Hennepin County. She only had one more check coming before her benefit would kick in.

Grandma Essie's desktop computer was painstakingly slow. Alana gasped as the login screen finally came into view. It was a picture of Grandma Essie standing next to her fully-decorated Christmas tree last year. The list of passwords was written on a notecard that she always kept in the center drawer of the desk. Alana searched the drawer and found the card. She stared at the image on the screen again for a moment then logged in by clicking on three specific ornaments on the picture. When the next screen emerged, she clicked on the big E on the toolbar. She sighed with impatience, waiting for the AOL home page to materialize. As soon as it came up, she noticed there were quite a few emails waiting to be read.

There might something important that needs to be answered, she thought as she clicked on the small envelope in the upper right on the screen. A man's voice announcing the "You've got mail!" slogan greeted her. She couldn't help but laugh. It reminded her of her parents—they still used AOL too!

Most of the emails were related to Grandma Essie's genealogy group and the local historical society. She began to scroll through them one by one until she came to one from a realtor offering to buy the house. The man was from a different agency than the one who'd showed up today. Then she found another email, and another, and another. All from the same person. As she read through them, the way the realtor kept stressing that he had an anxious buyer gave her pause.

Why would someone be champing at the bit to buy this house? Yes, it's unique and had been grand at one time, but there are similar homes in much better shape than this one for sale in town.

She performed a search of the realtor's name and found the nationwide company he represented in Faribault, Minnesota, about a half hour southeast of Merrick.

She went back and studied the emails, hoping to understand why his client was so obsessed with buying her grandma's house, but the messages were brief and didn't give the prospective buyer's name or his reason for the urgency to purchase this particular property. She clicked on the "Sent" file and found the information she'd been searching for in one of the last emails Grandma Essie had typed. It was dated two days before her death.

Dear Mr. Eldridge,

I am not interested in selling my house so please stop contacting me on behalf of your client. That has been my position all along and I'm not going to change my mind so I would appreciate it if you and your client would stop harassing me. He does not want to take no for an answer even though I have repeatedly made it very clear that I will not sell to him or anyone else.

This is the last time you are going to hear from me. If this harassment does not stop, I will contact my attorney to send you both a cease and desist letter.

Sincerely,

Mrs. Essie Anderson

Alana's heart began to slam in her chest. This was it—the smoking gun Reid was looking for and from the content of this email, the situation definitely *was* more serious than anyone had realized. With shaking hands, she picked up Grandma Essie's landline and tried to punch in Reid's private number, but her grip was so wobbly she dropped the handset. She caught her breath and picked it up again, managing to punch in the numbers from the sticky note on the corner of her desk.

When he answered, he seemed to immediately sense her anxiety. "Alana? Is something wrong?"

"Yes. There's something you need to see. Get over here. Now!"

***

"C'mon, sweetie. Sit still so Daddy can put your shoes on."

Hannah wiggled with impatience as Reid struggled to slip on her tennis shoes without untying them first. The first one went on with ease. The second one was tied too tight and wouldn't go on her foot.

"Here," he said giving up. "Hold your shoe." He handed it to her." I'll put it on later." He scooped her into his arms. "We're leaving."

"Where are we going?" Hannah asked quizzically as he hurried through the living room. "To get a happy meal?"

"We're going to Alana's house." He slammed the kitchen door shut and hurried through the screen porch.

62

"Can she come too? I'm hungry!"

Reid hustled down the back steps and crossed the yard, hoping Alana had something for Hannah to snack on. It was getting close to dinnertime and Hannah tended to get cranky when she needed to eat. He looked up. The leaden sky and sultry air indicated it was going to rain sometime tonight.

"I dropped my shoe!"

"Never mind about that, honey," Reid said as he speed-walked through the open gate of the picket fence dividing their yards. "We'll get it on the way back home." He sprinted up the back steps and burst into Alana's kitchen, finding her standing at the counter, opening a bottle of wine. Her hands shook uncontrollably.

"Here, let me do that," he said as he put Hannah down. "You're shaking like a leaf."

"It's a little early for a drink, but I need something to calm my nerves."

"Why?" He took the bottle of Chianti Classico and the wine key from her hands. He remembered seeing it in a small wine rack in Essie's dining room. "What happened?"

As if to fortify herself, she braced her hands against the counter. "I fired up Grandma Essie's computer to get set up for unemployment and job searching when I found a bunch of unread emails. One thing led to another and pretty soon I found a series of emails from a realtor in Faribault who says his client is anxious to buy this house."

Reid's hands stilled. "Who is his client?"

"I don't know. He didn't divulge that information in any of the emails."

Reid pulled the foil off the bottle and began to screw the wine key into the cork. "Did you call the realtor and find out who it was?"

"No," she said, sounding irritated. "I called *you*. I thought you'd want to read the emails and get all the information before I did that."

"Good call. I do." He stared at her as he extracted the cork with a loud popping noise. "So, does this mean you're joining me in the search for Essie's attacker? Your dad came over yesterday and talked to me about giving you a hand with the roofing estimates. He told me you were sticking around for a few weeks to oversee the repairs and get the house ready to sell."

She gave him a long, serious look. "Do you really want my help? On the investigation, I mean."

He couldn't pull his gaze away, finding himself mesmerized by the softness of her wide amber eyes. "I can't think of anyone else I'd want on my team."

"Okay…" She stared deeply into his eyes. "But we need to keep what we're doing under the radar. My parents would be vehemently against it if they knew what we were up to, especially my dad. He believes such matters are best left to the police to handle and he'd argue that I was getting myself into a dangerous situation."

"I understand his concern," Reid said as he poured the wine into a pair of stemmed glasses on the counter, "and I agree. If we fail to find any concrete evidence, we'll know we gave it our best effort and simply let it go. If we prove our hunch, we'll take our case to the authorities for review."

Hannah pulled on the hem of his polo shirt. "I'm hungry. I want a Happy Meal!"

"I can't stay long," he said to Alana. "She needs her dinner every night at the same time or she gets cranky." As soon as he cleaned up the kitchen from dinner, he'd give Hannah a bath and put her to bed. Then he'd have the rest of the night to relax. The peacefulness of a quiet evening was one of life's little pleasures…

Alana leaned forward and smiled at Hannah. "How about a cookie? They're not homemade, but they'll do in a pinch." At Hannah's nod, she turned and pulled an opened package of Oreos from an upper cabinet.

"My weakness," she said to Reid. "I have one every night with a cup of decaf."

He held up his wineglass. "Let's let this Chianti breathe a bit while we take a quick look at those emails."

They went into the parlor, the room Essie used as her office. In the corner, an oscillating fan on a pedestal scattered a welcome breeze around the room. Essie didn't have even so much as a window air-conditioner and had been against buying one. She had liked the summer heat.

Alana sat down to the computer. She brought up the email program and opened the first one from the realtor, a man by the name of Mr. Eldridge. As they read the email together, Reid rested his hand on the back of her chair for support and leaned closer to read the screen, his arm lightly pressing against her shoulder. The deep, sultry aroma of her fragrance filled his nostrils, making it difficult to concentrate on reading the words. He swallowed hard and tried to focus on the content of the email.

"They all pretty much say the same thing," Alana said as she closed it out and opened the second one. "I've copied down his phone number."

Reid glanced at the time at the lower right corner of the screen. "Maybe you should give him a call and set up a time to meet."

She turned her head to reply and as their gazes held, his breath quickened.

"Okay," she said slowly, as though mesmerized by their closeness. Her eyes widened; her gaze dropped, focusing on his mouth. He leaned closer and angled his head, his lips nearly touching hers, but before he had a chance to kiss her, she suddenly pulled back. "No. I can't do this to Jemma. It's not right."

He wanted to argue that this moment wasn't about Jemma, but Hannah interrupted him.

"I want another one!" Hannah tugged on her hand. "I want another cookie!"

Alana quickly looked away and pushed back her chair. "Okay, I'll get you one." She stood and picked up her wineglass. "While I'm gone," she said to him in a business-like manner, "why don't you look at the email Grandma Essie sent in response to Mr. Eldridge's numerous requests?" She pulled a sheet of paper from the printer with her free hand and held it out to him. "I've printed it out to make sure we have a copy of it to give to the police."

Settling down, he took a deep breath and read Essie's email while Alana took Hannah into the kitchen for another cookie. From the distressed tone of Essie's words, it was easy to discern how deeply both this realtor and his client had upset her.

Things are starting to make better sense now, he thought as Essie's remark about being taken advantage of crossed his mind. If these men had treated her unfairly in any way, they would answer to him. If he found proof that one of them had murdered her, they'd get more than they'd bargained for…

Alana came back into the parlor with Hannah in tow and avoided his gaze, acting as though the near-kiss between them had never happened. Setting down her wineglass, she picked up Essie's landline, switched to speakerphone and dialed Mr. Eldridge's office number. His assistant answered and indicated he was currently out of town, but she made an appointment for Alana to see him at the end of the week.

"I'm disappointed to hear he's not available, but at least we got an appointment to speak with him," Alana said to Reid as she hung up the phone. "That's all we can do for now."

"I was hoping we'd get in to see him sooner than that, too, but it'll give us time to think about how we want to handle this meeting and what questions to ask." He finished his wine then leaned down and pulled Hannah into his arms, resting her against his chest. "I'd better get her home and make dinner before she gets too tired to eat."

Hannah finished her cookie and held out her hand for another one.

"No more treats for you, sweetie," Alana said softly to Hannah. "You'll spoil your dinner."

Hannah kept leaning away from Reid with her arms outstretched. "I want that!"

Alana looked confused. "What?" She turned toward a stack of toys on the parlor table. "This?" She pointed toward a stuffed bear, but Hannah kept focusing on something else; an old, worn doll. "Oh, you want *this*?" She held it up. "My old Cabbage Patch doll?"

Reid tried to pull Hannah's arms down but she fought him and kept reaching for the doll. "That doesn't belong to you, Hannah. You can't just demand someone else's property."

"That's okay. She can have it," Alana said amicably and handed Hannah the fat, brown-haired toy with chubby features.

Hannah grabbed the faded doll and clutched it tightly in her arms. Reid looked at Alana. "Are you sure?"

"Yes. If it makes her happy then she can keep it." Alana laughed. "I don't know where it came from. It was used when I got it. Grandma Essie probably bought it for me at a garage sale. She liked to pick up all kinds of unique things that way."

"Her name is Dolly Lisa," she said to Hannah. "I've got the papers for her."

Hannah didn't respond. She just kept hugging the doll.

Loud thunder rumbled overhead as a cool breeze suddenly ruffled the curtains in the open parlor window. Reid carried Hannah into the kitchen and proceeded to the back door.

"Don't forget her other shoe," Alana said and handed him the one Hannah had worn into the house. "Do you remember where you dropped it?"

He stopped at the door, not wanting to leave. "She dropped it at the gate. I'll take her home then go back and get it."

He opened the door and held it for a moment, wanting to say more to her than simply goodbye. Something furry squeezed through the opening and rushed into the kitchen. "Oh-oh, I accidentally let the dog in," he said as Dusty sashayed around the table, overjoyed to be in their company. "Sorry about that."

"It's all right," Alana said as she petted her shaggy, wiggly friend. "It's going to storm pretty soon and I can't see making her stay on the porch in bad weather, no matter what my mother says." She looked up. "Judging by the way she scooted into the house when the thunder started, I think she must be terrified of storms."

The sound of heavy raindrops splattered against the windows. Reid pushed the door open farther. "I'd better get going before we get soaked. Talk to you tomorrow."

He paused as she stared into his eyes. "Come over again when you get a chance," she said, "and we'll go over our game plan for when we meet Mr. Eldridge."

Then she got busy closing the kitchen windows.

He hurried home, wondering if she really meant that or if she was just being polite.

Chapter Six

Alana started up Grandma Essie's '94 Buick Roadmaster Estate Wagon and rolled down the driver's side window. The air-conditioning hadn't worked for years. Slowly, carefully, she backed it out of the garage then shifted the car into PARK. It was a tight fit inside the one-car, detached garage behind the house. The beige vehicle was as long as a barge with four doors and a rear hatch. Fancy vinyl panels along the exterior sides stretched from front to back and resembled light-colored driftwood. She got out, closed the hinged garage doors then opened the door to the back seat. "Come on, Dusty. Get in. We're going for a ride."

Dusty practically flew through the opening and jumped around on the leather seat, panting from the unusually hot and humid weather they'd been having. Alana rolled the passenger window down four inches, shut the door and got back into the driver's seat. Dusty whined and stuck her nose in Alana's ear.

"Hey, you're going to have a great day so quit fussing. You're going to the doggie parlor!"

Alana had arranged to meet Jemma for lunch at the Chinese restaurant in town and it just so happened that the groomer was right next door. Yesterday, when she'd made the appointment, the receptionist told her to drop Dusty off at nine in the morning and pick up the dog at three that afternoon. She wasn't meeting Jemma until eleven, but she had a bunch of errands to do anyway, like buy a stack of plastic storage containers at the local hardware store and find out where her parents' storage unit was located in the mini-storage facility on the edge of town.

Dusty cried loudly with separation anxiety when Alana carried her into the shop and handed her off to an attendant to place her in a large kennel. Feeling sad at having to leave her, Alana turned and quickly left the shop before she could change her mind.

She'll be happy when I come back to get her. She's going to look and feel like a new dog.

Alana had arranged for Dusty to get a flea bath and have all of the knotted clumps of old winter hair sheared off the dog's hind legs and bushy tail. Granted, she shouldn't be spending her last dime on a doggie beauty appointment, but since she currently couldn't afford her regular visit to her own hairdresser, at least she could get one for the dog. It was only a fraction of what she usually spent on herself, and it would make a world of difference in the dog's well-being. No more clumps of old, dirty hair on the kitchen floor and no more incessant scratching. Best of all, her mother couldn't object to having the dog in the house.

She met Jemma at eleven, sharp, at the House of Wong on Main Street, across from the public parking lot. They both arrived at the same time and entered the restaurant together. The familiar aromas of egg rolls and fried rice filled the air as they walked through the glass front door into a large room adorned with potted bamboo trees, intricate murals of dragons on the walls and brightly colored paper lanterns hanging from the ceiling.

"Let's have a cocktail first." Jemma laughed in her usual hearty way as she slid into her side of the booth and accepted her menu from the hostess. They had originally planned to meet for happy hour and dinner, but since they were both so busy, they'd decided on a luncheon instead.

Today Jemma wore a full-length beige skirt with wide, tiered ruffles that angled upward toward one hip. Her floral print blouse had a V-neck gathered by long, tasseled drawstrings. The heavy humidity had curled her long copper hair in tight ringlets.

"Your server will be right with you," the hostess said before she returned to the front desk to answer the phone.

When their server arrived, they ordered drinks then opened their menus.

Alana scanned the huge list of dishes offered. Too many choices. "What's good here? What do you recommend? The wonderful smell in this place makes me really hungry."

Jemma's mixture of beaded and gold bracelets jingled as she held up the menu and pointed to a section. "I like these—the combination plates."

Alana studied the list and decided on the one with cashew chicken, fried rice and a crispy egg roll. She closed her menu. "So, what's new with you?"

Jemma closed hers as well. "I've still got a lot to do to get ready for school to start next week. I've got most of my crafts planned for fall, but I haven't finished collecting all of the supplies I'll need. How is your packing going?"

Alana sighed. "Well, I've started…" She told Jemma about losing her job and agreeing to stay on in the house for a few more weeks to supervise the repairs.

The waitress reappeared with their drinks and took their lunch orders.

"I'm sad to hear that the house will be sold this fall," Jemma said quietly as she sipped her wine. "It's all happening so fast. I hope whoever purchases it will be as good of a neighbor as Essie was. I'll miss sitting in her kitchen, eating her homemade goodies at Christmastime."

"Me, too," Alana replied. She smiled, trying to lighten the conversation. "But when we're finished with the repairs, it'll be a beautiful house again. I doubt if it will take long to sell once we put it on the market."

"I'd love to buy it myself." Jemma gave her a wistful look. "Unfortunately, I couldn't afford it on my salary. I don't mind living with my parents, but it would be nice to have a place of my own." She absently slid her fingers down the stem of her glass. "Then I'd be living right next door to Reid."

"He's a good man. Grandma Essie was lucky to have him as a neighbor."

Jemma stiffened. "How would you know that?"

Alana faltered, confused by Jemma's sudden change in demeanor. "He and I have talked several times since I arrived at the house."

"When did you meet him? I should have been there." Jemma demanded, acting as though she found Alana's interaction with Reid a threat to her relationship with him. "I told you *I'd* introduce you."

Feeling cautious, Alana recounted the basic facts surrounding the day she'd stormed into his yard to find out why he'd sprayed Dusty and got doused with cold water herself.

"Well, I'm sure he didn't do it on purpose!"

"No, and I didn't mean to imply that," Alana replied evenly. "The next day I saw him again and he apologized for his mistake. Hannah had wandered into my yard so I brought her home." She purposely left out the part where he had asked for a truce because he wanted to become friends. If Jemma found their mere acquaintance threatening, how would she react if she discovered that several days ago, he'd spent time at her house...and almost kissed her?

Flooded with guilt, a sudden flush heated her cheeks. She and Jemma were lifelong friends. She had no business playing kissy face with the man Jemma had her heart set on, even if Reid didn't consider their relationship in the same way Jemma did. Alana had sworn off men to concentrate on her career and now that goal was more important than ever. She needed to get focused and take care of business.

But what about the fact that Reid and I are working together on Essie's case?

She couldn't let that opportunity go. It was too important. Nothing must get in the way of investigating Grandma Essie's horrible death. Until she and Reid were ready to go to the police, no one must know of their plan. In the meantime, she vowed to keep her distance when she was around him—both physically and emotionally.

Jemma looked visibly upset that she'd been left out. "What else did you and he talk about?"

"Not much. He was busy grilling burgers."

Jemma looked like she'd been blindsided. "Knowing Reid, he asked you to stay for dinner. Why wasn't *I* invited?"

The desperate tone in Jemma's voice made Alana uncomfortable. She swallowed hard at Jemma's unexpected reaction to such an innocent and totally unplanned situation. "I don't know. It was last minute—no big deal." She shrugged. "I had a burger and went home." Well, there was a little more to it than that, but it served no good purpose to reveal anything else they spoke about.

Jemma's eyes narrowed, showing a side to her that Alana had never seen before. Or had she simply overlooked it because Jemma had never turned on her until now? "Reid is *my* man, Alana. I get that you're probably lonely without Dylan, but if you're sizing up Reid as your next conquest, *look somewhere else.*"

"I—I'm not. I mean, I wouldn't..." Stunned, Alana froze, not knowing what to say.

Thankfully, their waitress appeared at the table with their lunch plates, providing a timely distraction. Alana quickly busied herself digging into her hot food; it was delicious, but she didn't enjoy it like she had originally anticipated. Instead, Jemma's animosity toward her had troubled her and made her anxious to leave. Jemma obviously held the same feelings. She ate half of her food in stony silence then asked for a container to take the rest home. Alana did the same.

They paid the bill and left the restaurant. Without turning around, Jemma murmured goodbye on her way out and headed across the parking lot to her car. Alana stood at the door of the doggie salon and, with a heavy heart, watched her best friend swiftly walk away. After today, she didn't know what their status was. Were they even on speaking terms anymore?

I need to fix this, she thought sadly. *Reid's an attractive guy in many ways, but he isn't worth the loss of my best friend. Jemma and I have been like sisters most of our lives. I hope we can repair our relationship over this misunderstanding...*

She went into the busy salon filled with yowling dogs missing their owners and the sound of blow dryers fluffing canine coats. The receptionist asked her a question, but her mind was so distracted she didn't hear it.

"I know I'm early," she said to the receptionist, hoping she'd given the right answer, "but I'll just wait for Dusty."

"Actually, she's ready now," the young, dark-haired woman replied.

Alana paid the bill and followed a groomer to a back room where dogs waited in square kennels for their owners. The moment Dusty heard her voice, the dog began to bark and whine.

"Well, look at you," Alana exclaimed as she waited for the groomer to open the kennel door and scoop up the dog. Dusty had a gleaming coat that smelled like gardenias, a new flea collar with a red satin bow fastened to it, small red bows fastened to the fur atop each of her ears and red-painted toenails. The groomer carried the dog to the front desk then handed her off to Alana.

"Come on, baby, let's go home," Alana said as she took the dog in her arms and left the salon.

She didn't have a leash so she carried Dusty to her car and opened the passenger door, placing the dog inside. As she walked around to the driver's side, Dusty jumped about on the seat, wiggling her body as hard as she could to let Alana know how happy she was to be clean and on her way home. It made Alana realize why dogs were called 'Man's Best Friend.'

Sadly, right now, Dusty felt like her only friend in Merrick, Minnesota.

***

Reid hung up the phone, his ears still burning from Nate's lecture on meeting his deadlines. Nate had voiced his concerns—in detail—about the numerous situations Reid had allowed himself to get tangled up in and distract him. He'd complained it was slowing down Reid's progress.

Reid stood at the window, thinking about all of the tasks he needed to finish before his next conference in a few weeks when a contractor's truck pulled up to the front of Essie's house and added one more. Two men got out wearing beige work uniforms, one younger and one older. They began discussing something as they looked up at the tarp-covered roof.

Hannah had just gone down for a nap and was fast asleep in her bed, curled up under a worn baby quilt and clutching her doll when Reid checked on her. He stepped out the front door into the sweltering heat and walked over to the men. He introduced himself, explained his purpose for being there and shook hands with both. The men were father and son, owners of a roofing company that Darren Morgan had contacted for an estimate.

"Darren and Terra live in the Twin Cities so it's tough for them to get down here on short notice. I'm handling the bidding process for them."

"Sure, no problem. He spoke to me about that when he contacted me for the estimate," Harlan, the older, gray-haired man, said. Ed, the younger one with reddish hair, grabbed his metal clipboard while Harlan brought up the location of the house on Google Earth to get an aerial view. They went into the backyard and stood under a large shade tree next to the garage, talking at length about dimensions, recommended shingles and a "tear off" versus applying new shingles over the old ones to fix the deterioration underneath.

They were finishing up when Alana pulled into the crushed rock driveway in Essie's old Buick. The men stared at her vintage car as she drove it up to the garage and got out, remarking what amazing shape it was in. As she approached the group, the men introduced themselves, referring to her as Mrs. Sinclair.

She laughed, though her face blushed profusely. "We're not married. Reid lives next door. My parents are the owners."

"That's too bad," Harlan said with a jovial ring in his voice. "You two make a nice-looking couple."

Reid cleared his throat and changed the subject, asking how long it would take to get the estimate. Harlan indicated he'd email it to Reid within a few days.

The men thanked them for the opportunity to bid on the house, got into their truck and left.

"Well, that's two down," Reid said with a sigh and turned to Alana. "One more to go. I told Darren he should get three bids."

Then I've got to get back to work on my own projects…

"Da-dee…"

Reid spun around to find Hannah walking across the yard, clutching her doll and rubbing one eye. "She didn't get much of a nap," he said wearily. "The loud engine of that truck must have awakened her." He scooped her into his arms and she buried her face in his shoulder, whimpering. "Come on, princess. You need to go back to bed."

Hannah let out a tired wail and began to kick her feet.

"Why don't we take a walk around the yard?" Alana offered. "Maybe the steady motion will calm her down and put her back to sleep."

She leaned close to Hannah and brushed a curl from her face. "Is that okay, Hannah? Do you want to take a walk with me and your daddy?"

Hannah quit crying immediately. Without looking up, she sniffled and nodded her head.

She's so patient with my daughter, he marveled to himself. *I wish Hannah would have been blessed with a mother like her.*

They walked the length of Essie's large yard toward her back porch, discussing several helpful comments the contractor made about replacing the roof. In the meantime, Hannah closed her eyes and quickly fell back to sleep.

"Why don't you lay her in the hammock on the porch," Alana suggested. "We can turn on the fan and sit in the lawn chairs and talk."

Reid gently laid Hannah in the center of the soft, old hammock suspended from the ceiling and waited a few moments to make sure she was still asleep.

Alana unlocked the back door and gently pushed it open. Dusty bounded out of the kitchen and raced down the steps, happy to be outdoors. Alana stepped into the kitchen and returned with a tall, oscillating fan. "Would you like something to drink?" She plugged in the fan to an outside outlet and set it on low. "I've still got some of that wine left." Her voice was friendly, but the aloofness in her manner warned him something had changed between them.

"Not in this heat." Reid laughed, making an attempt to act like he didn't notice. "How about a cola?"

She paused. "Is a Diet Pepsi okay? That's all I've got."

"Works for me."

She disappeared into the kitchen again and returned a couple minutes later with the sodas and ice-filled glasses. They sat in silence for a little while as they drank their beverages. Dusty had settled at Alana's feet, panting from the heat.

Reid drained his glass and set it on a small table. "I don't know what you did to Dusty, but it's a fantastic improvement. She doesn't look like the same dog."

Alana smiled. "I took her to the groomer in town. It's amazing what a medicated shampoo and a good trim will do."

"Sounds like you're planning to keep her."

"I'd like to, but she'd have to live in a condo in downtown Minneapolis. It doesn't sound like a good fit for either of us." She looked troubled, but he had a hunch it had nothing to do with the dog.

"Alana, about the other night—"

"Reid, I—"

He held up his hand. "You go first."

She placed her hands in her lap and sat back in her chair. "I had lunch with Jemma yesterday."

"Oh?" Tension twisted the muscles in the back of his neck. "How'd that go?"

She glanced over at him. "I think you already know the answer to that."

Worried, he leaned forward. "Give me the details."

"In a nutshell, she and I can't be friends as long as you and I are *neighborly* toward one another. She got very upset when she learned that we had already met and spoken to each other several times without her knowledge. In so many words, she accused me of chasing after you because we ate a burger together."

He let out a tense sigh. "This is getting ridiculous. She and I are *not* a couple, Alana. We're only friends and after this—"

"Yes, well, Jemma and I *are* friends and have been since we were preschoolers. I like you, Reid, but I'm caught in the middle between the two of you. I don't know why she's gone all weird on me like this, but if I have to choose between you and her, I choose her."

Alana's senseless capitulation to Jemma's demands made him angry. "Backing off completely, are you? So, no more investigation then?"

Hannah stirred, causing both of them to go silent for a few moments. Alana folded her arms and stared at the floor, her jaw set.

"I still want that," she said at last, holding her voice low, "as long as we continue to keep it secret. I'm as serious about uncovering the truth concerning Grandma Essie's death as you are, but what I *don't* want is to upset my best friend more than I already have. So yes, I'm backing off in that respect. I value my friendship with Jemma."

She stared at him, the guilt in her eyes conveying what she

considered the ultimate betrayal to Jemma—not that he'd tried to kiss her, but that she'd *wanted* him to kiss her...

"When we conclude this investigation and my work on the house is done here," Alana stated solemnly, "I'm going back to Minneapolis to get on with my life. That's where my home is, where my next job will be located and where I belong."

"And Jemma?"

"She'll meet the right man someday and find her happily ever after. In the meantime, I don't plan to be in her way."

Neither will I, starting immediately...

He needed to have a serious, long-overdue talk with Jemma and if need be, end their friendship no matter how awkward it would be going forward. Nate was right; it was high time he realigned his priorities and got back on track with his life.

He expelled a wry laugh. "Jemma is a lot like my agent. Nate has no trouble finding a girlfriend, but he's so jealous and controlling he can't seem to keep one."

Alana gave him a droll smile. "Maybe you should get those two together. It might be a match made in heaven."

"Not in a million years..." Reid shook his head. "I'm no matchmaker, especially when it comes to Nate. He can find his own women."

She set down her glass. "As far as the investigation is concerned, where do we go from here?"

"Glad you asked." Reid stood up. "We've never scoured this property for clues. I know it's been over a month and the storms have probably washed everything away, but you never know, we could be missing something that's right in plain sight."

Alana stood and glanced down at Hannah slumbering peacefully in the hammock. "She should be all right napping here. If she awakens, we'll be close by to make sure she doesn't roll out."

They began a search by advancing from the house to the edge of the property, one footstep at a time, but after thoroughly checking both the front and back yards, their quest turned up empty.

"This is so disappointing," Alana complained as she wiped her brow. "We've covered every inch—for nothing." She looked down at her smudged legs. "It was no fun crawling under the porch looking for evidence, either." She shivered with revulsion. "I encountered a lot of bugs under there."

Reid glanced around. "Maybe we should check the path."

Alana gave him a dubious look. "It's muddy and slippery from the rain. *You* can do that. I'll stay at the top of the hill. Someone needs to keep an eye on Hannah."

They walked to the path and Alana kept watch as Reid maneuvered his way down the slope, looking for something that might be useful to their investigation. The ground was so slick he nearly lost his footing several times, but was able to grab onto low-hanging tree limbs to keep himself upright.

Growing tired, he stepped off the path into the brush to catch his breath and looked down to monitor his footing. Not far away, he saw a small patch of white among the decomposing leaves on the ground. Curious, he plowed through the brush and picked it up. It was a soggy business card. He flipped it over.

"Dan Eldridge," he said aloud, sounding as surprised as he felt. "Well, what do you know..."

He looked around some more, spreading out the leaves and rocks with his hands and found a small piece of black nylon string, like the one on Essie's medical alert necklace.

Alana had stepped away to check on Hannah but she suddenly

appeared at the top of the slope. "Did you find anything?"

"Maybe," he replied tentatively. Making his way back through the brush, he laid a branch across the path to mark the spot before walking up the slope and rejoining her. He reached the top of the hill and held out the soggy card. "Look at this."

She examined it and gasped. "Where did you find it?"

He pointed down the slope. "Over there, in the brush. And I found this, too." He held out the fragment of nylon string. "I don't know for sure, but it looks like part of Essie's medical alert necklace. I'm going back with a rake to see if I can find the device."

They walked back to the yard and found a leaf rake in the garage. Reid went back down the path and searched the area once more, digging through the leaves with the metal rake. After a few minutes, he rejoined Alana.

"Did you find anything else?"

He held out his palm containing small fragments of white plastic. "If this was her necklace, it was totally destroyed."

Alana clutched her hands over her heart. "He wanted to make sure she couldn't use it to call for help." She looked up. "But why smash it to pieces when he could have simply thrown it in the trash? It seems like an angry gesture to me."

Reid closed his palm. "Maybe it was. Maybe killing her for refusing to sell wasn't enough." He stared at the business card in Alana's hand. "When we meet this guy tomorrow, I'm going to look him straight in the eye. If he did it, I'll know right away."

Alana squeezed his arm, a hopeful, but worried look in her beautiful amber eyes. "Please, be careful."

Chapter Seven

The next morning, Alana stored her Mercedes in the garage and drove the Buick a half hour southeast to the town of Lonsdale to meet Reid. He needed to pick up a printed copy of his manuscript at the office supply store so they agreed to converge there. She drove the station wagon into the store parking lot next to his red Chrysler Pacifica and waited for him. He emerged from the store a few minutes later leading Hannah with one hand and carrying a flat brown bag with the other.

Alana jumped out of her car and met him at the passenger side of his SUV. She opened the door and got in while he settled Hannah snugly in her safety seat.

"Lana!" Hannah cried excitedly. "I get a Happy Meal!"

Alana turned in the front seat and smiled. "You do? Isn't that fun!"

Hannah's long curly hair hung in ringlets past her shoulders. Her head bobbed up and down like it was on a spring. "And a toy too!"

"What time are you having lunch?"

Hannah thought for a moment and shrugged.

"You have to be a good girl when we go to our appointment," Reid said as he buckled the seatbelt holding her car seat. "No running around or fussing. All right? Just sit on Daddy's lap and when we're finished, we'll go straight to McDonald's. Okay?"

"Oh-kay." Hannah nodded while she spoke, smiling from ear to ear.

Reid pulled on the buckle to make sure it was secure then shut the car door and rounded the vehicle. He slipped into to the driver's seat and gave Alana a 'thumbs up.' "So far, so good, but I have reinforcements, just in case." He pointed to a busy bag on the floor next to her feet filled with small toys, fruit and other healthy snacks.

They pulled into the realty parking lot at ten-fifty for their eleven o'clock appointment.

"We're here to see Mr. Eldridge," Reid said to the receptionist as they approached the front desk.

"I'll let him know you're here." The young blonde motioned toward a line of upholstered chairs in the reception area. "Have a seat. He'll be out to meet you shortly."

Hannah immediately became enamored with the fish tank and stood in fascination watching a vivid blue angelfish flutter up and down next to the glass.

Mr. Eldridge kept them cooling their heels for fifteen minutes. When he appeared in the lobby to meet them, he was cordial, but he approached them with caution, as though he already suspected the reason for their visit. Tall, thin and white-haired, the older man wore a tailored gray business suit and matching tie over a white shirt.

Alana and Reid took turns shaking hands with him and introducing themselves. Dan Eldridge led them into his office and shut the door. "Please have a seat." He sat down behind his large desk. "So, what can I do for you?"

Taking a deep breath, Alana folded her hands in her lap to project an image of calm—the opposite of her current feelings. "I'm interested in possibly listing my grandmother's house with your agency," she began. "She recently passed away and I'm in the process of getting it ready to sell."

"My apologies on the death of you grandmother," he said kindly.

"Thank you, Mr. Eldridge."

"Just call me Dan."

"It was a shock to all of us, especially my mother, but she's doing as well as can be expected," she continued. "My parents live in the Twin Cities and they have other pressing business right now so Reid and I are handling most of the work for them."

"We understand," Reid said, shifting Hannah on his lap, "that you have a client who is already interested in the house. The late Mrs. Anderson briefly mentioned it to me one day when she was caring for my daughter. That's why we decided to contact you."

For a moment, Dan Eldridge's eyes narrowed slightly, as though Reid had touched upon a sensitive subject, but he recovered quickly. "He asked me to contact Mrs. Anderson on his behalf, but nothing ever came of it. I'm no longer in communication with that buyer."

Why not? Alana noticed the abrupt change in his tone and wanted to know more. "If you'd be so kind as to give us his name, we'll contact him ourselves."

"That won't be possible," Dan responded in a steely-soft voice. "I'm sorry, but that information is confidential."

"All right then," Reid persisted, "would you contact him for us and ask him to give me a call?"

"I don't believe he's in the area any longer." Dan leaned forward. "Mr. Sinclair, I'll have no trouble whatsoever finding prospective buyers, if that's a concern to you. The late Mrs. Anderson's house is a beautiful specimen of Queen Anne architecture and it'll sell for a terrific price." He shifted his focus to Alana. "If you'd like, I'll contact your parents today to draw up a listing agreement."

It was obvious they weren't going to get any information out of him. They were wasting both their time and his. "I'd prefer to discuss the matter with them first," she said and reached down for her handbag. "If they agree, I'll have them give you a call."

Dan stood and handed her a business card, thanking them for stopping by. The meeting was over.

They left the realty in silence. Once they were seated in the car, Reid turned to her. "He didn't do it."

Alana grabbed her seatbelt and shoved the metal fitting into the buckle. "I knew it right way, and I was disappointed he wouldn't cooperate with us when we asked about his so-called *confidential* client." She looked up. "He seemed awfully nervous about the entire situation to me."

"Yeah." Reid pulled out his sunglasses and slipped them on. "I'll bet I know why…"

"He suspects his client might have something to do with Essie's death."

"Yep. I could sense it all over him." Reid started the SUV and turned the air-conditioning on full blast. "The more I think about it, the more I want to find out who this mystery guy is."

"I'm disappointed this lead turned out to be a dead end. Now what do we do?"

"Well," Reid replied as he drove out of the parking lot, "first, we stop at McDonalds and get Hannah's Happy Meal, then we go to a full-service restaurant, order a cold beverage and plan our next move. How do you feel about Mexican food? I know a place here in Faribault that serves the best fajitas." He grinned. "My treat."

Alana smiled. "As long as they're preceded by a frosty margarita, I'm game."

He pulled onto the highway. "Your wish is my command."

***

Thirty minutes later, Alana sipped a margarita and munched on chips and salsa while she and Reid waited for their food to arrive. Hannah sat quietly next to Reid, stuffing her face with apple slices and playing with her new toy.

"So, what's on your mind? Where does our investigation go from here?' Alana asked as she dipped a crisp, warm chip into a bowl of spicy salsa.

"I've been thinking..." Reid set down his drink. "The thing is, I could count on one hand the number of vehicles that showed up at Essie's house when she was alive. She kept the same schedule week in and week out and had the same visitors. I never saw any cars in front of her house or in her driveway that I didn't recognize." He rubbed his chin thoughtfully. "That means whoever kept coming to see her must have either walked or parked down the block. But if someone had parked along the street, it would have been in the gossip pipeline and Jemma would have told me about it."

Alana froze. "Are you thinking what I'm thinking?"

"He parked in the municipal lot and took the path."

"Right." She nodded. "No one would pay any attention to his car in a busy lot where people are constantly coming and going."

Reid went still and stared at his drink. His eyes suddenly narrowed. "I keep thinking about how that business card was so easy to find."

"Me, too." Alana wiped her lips on her napkin. "I wonder if he purposely left it there with the pieces of the medical alert to throw suspicion on Dan Eldridge."

"Well, if he did, it didn't work. We know Eldridge didn't kill Essie, but who did? There's only one way to find out."

"What is that? I just pointed out his advantage is that no one would notice him coming or going."

Reid sat back and folded his arms. "There is one possibility."

She waited for him to continue but he simply kept staring at his drink.

"*What?*"

"The guys in the city garage. They come and go, but there is someone there all the time—the supervisor of Public Works. His office overlooks the parking lot. If anyone noticed anything unusual, it would be him." Reid checked his watch. "It's too late to catch him today." He looked up. "I'll talk to him tomorrow."

She picked up a chip and flicked it at him. "Not without me."

"It's a date." He smiled. "Sort of."

***

"Anybody home?"

Reid stood on Essie's back porch holding Hannah in his arms. She'd just awakened from her nap and was still a little sleepy.

"Come on in," Alana called from the parlor. "I'll be right there."

He set Hannah down and opened the screen door. Dusty met them in the kitchen, wagging her tail and whining to be petted. Hannah put her arms around the dog's neck and gave her a hug.

Alana came through the living room and appeared in the kitchen doorway wearing cutoff jeans and a red and white top. Though it was cooler today, she'd wound her long, dark hair into a French braid.

Hannah forgot about Dusty and ran toward her. "Hi, Lana! Can I haf a cookie?"

"Of course, sweetie," she replied as she went to the cabinet and grabbed the Oreo package.

Reid held up his hand to stall the process. "What do you say, Hannah?"

Hannah smiled. "Pweeease!"

Alana handed her the cookie.

"Thank you!"

Reid turned to Alana. "How's the job search coming along? Make any progress this morning?"

She set the package on the counter. "I spent part of the time replacing the modem I bought yesterday in Faribault and getting my laptop connected to it. I've got accounts with a half-dozen job search engines and through them, I found a couple new openings in the Twin Cities. I've applied to over a dozen places so far, but no bites yet."

"How's that new modem working out?"

She laughed. "Like greased lightning compared to what was here. Grandma Essie's old computer was so unbearably slow I couldn't stand it. Some zealous salesperson at her internet provider had talked her into paying for wi-fi so her family could use it when they were here, but she'd never gotten around to figuring out how to use it herself." Her face clouded. "I should have taken the time to drive down here and help her out, but I guess I was too busy…"

"Hey," he said softly and squeezed her arm. "Don't beat yourself up over that. It didn't matter to her. I never once heard Essie say she needed a faster computer or that she wished she knew how to shop on her phone. She could have asked me for help if she'd wanted it."

"Sometimes I wish *I* didn't know how to shop on my phone." Alana laughed. "It's hard to resist, especially now." She picked her phone off the counter and shoved it in her pocket. "I'm ready to go any time you are," she said, changing the subject. "I just need to grab my purse from the other room and lock up."

The path was too steep to walk down carrying a small child so Reid drove them down to the parking area in his SUV. They parked and walked into the city garage, requesting to speak to the supervisor. A short, balding man wearing a dark blue work uniform appeared from one of the dingy offices in the front of the building. His plastic badge read simply, 'Al.'

He looked concerned as he approached them. "What can I do for you people?"

Alana took Hannah in her arms and held her as Reid introduced himself. "I'm looking for a guy who parks in the lot once in a while and walks up that path on the other end. Have you ever seen him?"

Al burst into a wide, toothy grin. "Oh, you mean the guy with the black Silverado pickup? The shiny one with chrome trim and tinted windows... Sure, I've seen him a few times, but not lately. Whatcha want with him?"

Don't sound too eager...

"Ah, I just want to talk to him. I heard the pickup was for sale and I thought I'd see what he was asking for it."

"Well, I wouldn't know about that. Jones might, though. He walked over to it once and checked it out." He turned toward one of the maintenance bays. "Hey, Jones! You seen that black Silverado around lately? The fella here says he heard it was for sale."

A muffled voice from the back of the shop answered him.

Al turned back to them. "Guess not."

Out of options, Reid shoved his hands into his pockets.

"Well, what does the owner look like?" Alana burst out. "In case we see him uptown."

Al shrugged. "Medium height, husky, dark-haired. That's about all I can tell from this distance."

"Thank you," Reid said. "You've been a great help." He handed Al his business card. "If you ever see that pickup truck again, I'd appreciate if you'd give me a call."

Al glanced briefly at the card and stuck it in his shirt pocket. "Sure 'ting, Mr. Sinclair."

They left the garage and walked back to the Pacifica.

"A black Silverado with chrome trim and tinted windows..." Reid said under his breath. "Pickup trucks are dime a dozen around here, but not one that classy. I'm surprised I haven't noticed it around town."

Alana gave him a sideways glance. "You weren't looking for it. Now you won't be able to miss it."

He held out his key fob and unlocked the car. "Let's hope..."

Chapter Eight

Later that day...

Alana took a break from her work and stood up, pressing her hands against the dull ache in her lower back. She'd spent several hours packing everything in the dining room—which meant cleaning out the curved china cabinet and the built-in buffet. Except for the table and chairs, the room now stood empty. Every noise she made echoed off the walls. She'd thoroughly emptied and cleaned four rooms so far, but that wasn't even half of the house. Then there was the attic and the basement and the garage. And the kitchen... that room was definitely going to be last.

She groaned aloud, just thinking about what she had left to finish.

She'd been so busy working, she hadn't realized she'd missed dinner. Her stomach made a gurgling noise, reminding her she hadn't eaten for hours. She went into the kitchen to heat up something quick, but all she could find was a can of chicken and rice soup. As she stood at the stove heating the soup, she thought about the dismal state of her finances. She still had about half of the money left that her father had given her, but that was disappearing fast. The Buick was a gas hog with a huge tank that took a chunk of cash to fill. But that was the least of her worries. Her bank account was shrinking more every day as automatic electronic payments were posted to pay her bills. If she didn't find a job pretty soon, her situation was going to turn dire…

She sighed and pushed the thought from her mind. It didn't do any good to worry about it.

"Something will turn up," she said aloud to assure herself. "It always does. In the meantime, I need to watch my spending."

Did I really just say that? I'm starting to sound like my parents…

Pinching pennies was something she'd never had to do before in her entire life and she hoped she'd never find herself in this situation ever again. For now, hair appointments, nail appointments, power shopping trips or weekend getaways with her girlfriends were indefinitely on hold. She had to conserve every dime she had left until she resumed getting regular paychecks once more. It made her all the more determined to get back to work.

Dusty lay on the braided rug by the kitchen door, waiting for her dinner as well. As soon as Alana set a dish of dog food on the floor, Dusty hurried over to it, wolfing it down in mere seconds. It made Alana sad to see how the dog still believed every morsel she ate might be her last and she wondered if Dusty would ever get over the fear going hungry.

She took her soup into the living room to read a magazine while she ate. It was overcast and chilly today; an indication that summer was giving way to fall. She'd just finished eating when heavy footsteps strode across the back porch. Dusty raised her head, her ears perked, listening intently. A low growl rumbled in her throat.

Strong fingers rapped on the kitchen door. Dusty sprang to her feet, barking loudly, a ridge of hair spiking along her spine.

Alana rose and went into the kitchen to answer the door. As she approached, a man's silhouette appeared behind the gather of a sheer curtain in the door's square glass window. Why was Reid coming over at this hour? It was nearly Hannah's bath time. He must have learned something he needed to tell her and it couldn't wait. She flipped on the porch light, grabbed the door handle and jerked it open. A cold wave of crisp, damp air wafted into the room and swirled around her, spreading goosebumps up her arms. "Reid, what's the mat—"

It wasn't Reid.

***

Dressed in solid black pants, shirt and blazer, the man stood about her height—five feet and nine inches. A gold Cartier watch glistened on his wrist under the bright LED light. Armani cologne shrouded him like an invisible cloak. His dark eyes studied her intently.

Medium height, husky and dark-haired—he fit the exact description Al had given her and Reid this afternoon. Alana's breath caught in her throat, her heart pounding in her chest. Her first instinct was to slam the door shut, but the size of his arms suggested it would be a futile move. Instead, she grabbed the dog by the collar and pulled her close. Dusty glared at him and growled. Alana hoped the dog's warning would convince him to keep his distance.

"Hello," he said in a deep, smooth voice. His generous smile was polite, but his gaze focused on her with an intensity that made her nervous. "I apologize for dropping by without an appointment, but I heard this house is for sale. I'm interested in purchasing it."

He's the one… she thought, panicking. *He pressured my grandma to sell and when she kept refusing…*

The thought frightened her.

"Do you mind if I come in and have a look around?" His voice had softened in an attempt to be charming, but she didn't fall for it and had no intention of letting him in.

Dragging the dog with her, she stepped onto the porch, hoping Reid would see them and come over to find out what was going on. "I'm in the middle of cleaning it out and the place is a mess. I'd rather not show it to anyone yet."

"How much are you asking for it?"

"I have no idea. It—it's not on the market yet and I don't know when it will be," she said, stumbling over her words. "That's up to my parents. They're the owners." She stayed in the doorway and gripped her fingers on the handle of the screen door as a subtle gesture for him to leave.

"Then I guess I need to speak to *them* instead," he said dismissively. His eyes hardened. "I'll need their phone number."

"They're not home. They left today on an extended trip to Europe and won't be back until the middle of October." She feigned a polite smile. "Give me your card and I'll pass it along to them when they get back."

In truth, they weren't leaving until the day after tomorrow, but he didn't need to know that. A few weeks ago, in preparation for their trip, her parents had added her name to their safety deposit box and given her a key. The box contained all of their important information, including notarized copies of their wills and individual powers of attorney for Alana in case anything should happen to them. She had the power to sell the house to him if she wanted to, but she had no intention of even discussing the possibility with him. She wanted him to leave.

He stared at her with laser-like precision. "Fine, I guess I'll have to wait, but I plan to buy this house, and in the meantime, I want to move in as soon as possible. Perhaps we could work out a temporary agreement to rent it until your parents return."

She shook her head. "I don't have the authority to make an agreement with you. Besides, the house needs major repairs first. Like a new roof for starters."

"I don't care about that," he countered, contradicting her argument with a wave of his hand. "I'll get everything fixed myself."

He seemed to have an answer for everything. She swallowed hard, trying to hold back her desperation. What would this guy do to her parents if they refused? Instead of looking him in the eye, her gaze focused on the sparkle of a large emerald-cut diamond in his left ear. "How did you know the house was for sale? Our realtor hasn't even put a sign on the lawn yet."

"This is a small town. Word travels fast…" He glanced around, as though checking to make sure no one was watching them. "Whatever you're asking for this place, I'll pay ten percent above that. In cash."

His obsession with getting this house was extremely troubling, but she concentrated on keeping her manner even. "That's between you and my parents. Leave your name and number and I'll have them call you."

He reached into his blazer pocket and pulled out a business card. "The next time you talk with them, tell them I'm anxious to speak to them and to work out a deal that will benefit us both." He handed it to her. "We don't need to get realtors involved. My lawyer will handle the closing," he said as he turned away. "I'll be in touch." He walked down the back steps, crossed the yard and disappeared down the path.

Alana shivered as she darted back into the kitchen with Dusty, slammed the door shut and locked it. Then she ran to the front door and made sure the deadbolt was set on that one, too. With shaking hands, she picked her phone off the kitchen table and dialed Reid's private number.

He answered on the third ring. "Hello," he said, sounding preoccupied. Voices from the television echoed in the background. "Hello? Who is this?"

"It's me," Alana said once she finally caught her breath.

"Alana?" His voice sounded concerned. The background noises suddenly went quiet. "What's wrong? Are you all right?"

"He was here…"

"Who? Who are you talking about?"

"He gave me his card. I didn't see his truck because he used the path, but I *know* he's the man with the black Silverado."

"At your house?" Reid sounded perplexed. "Is he still there?" Without waiting for an answer, he added, "I'll be right over!"

The line went dead.

***

Reid locked the door behind him and left the house as quietly as possible. Hannah was upstairs in bed and he'd just gotten her to sleep for the night. He didn't plan to be away long, but he also didn't want her waking up and wandering around looking for him while he was gone.

Once outside, he sprinted across the yard and dashed through the gate, running as fast as he could. He didn't have the speed he once had in high school when he'd competed in track, but he could still run fast for short distances. He practically flew onto Essie's back porch and tried to open the door, but it was locked. He pounded on the heavy oak frame. "Alana, it's Reid! Open Up!"

She flipped on the yard light and pulled back the sheer curtain. When she saw it was him, she turned the deadbolt lock and jerked open the door. Her face looked ashen. "All of a sudden he was in my face and said he wanted to buy the house—with cash—didn't care what shape it was in and wanted to move in right away...and...and..."

"Hey, hey." Reid covered her hands with his. A stranger whose mere presence had frightened her and who may very well be the same man who murdered Essie—the realization made his chest tighten with fear. Suddenly, his arms were around her, holding her close. "Slow down and take a deep breath." He placed his hand on the back of her head and gently pressed her cheek against his shoulder. "You're shivering," he whispered in her ear.

"I'm cold." Her teeth chattered as her arms latched around his neck. "And I'm...upset." After a moment she looked up. As their eyes met, she cleared her throat and lowered her arms to her sides. "I'll—I'll be fine."

"Let's go sit on the sofa so you can warm up." Reluctantly, he pulled his arms away, locked the door behind him and led her into the living room. He pulled a crocheted afghan off the sofa and wrapped it around her. "Now, start at the beginning."

She spent the next five minutes filling him in on as many details as she could remember, from the moment the man knocked on the door until he walked away from the porch.

"Who is he? Did he tell you his name?"

Alana shivered and pulled the afghan tighter around her. "He gave me this." She handed him a mangled business card.

Reid straightened it out and read aloud, "Richard Jeffers, private investor." He looked up. "If he's an investor, he probably wants to buy this house and flip it. He may already have a buyer."

Alana shook her head. "I don't get it. He said he'd pay ten percent over market value in cash and wanted to move in as soon as possible. He even wanted to rent it until the closing. He said he'd do the repairs himself."

"Of course," Reid said in a cynical tone. "He wants to buy it in its current rundown state, make basic repairs and flip it for a nice price." He pulled her to her feet. The afghan fell to a heap on the floor. "Go upstairs and pack a bag."

She looked confused. "Why?"

"Because you're coming home with me tonight." She tried to argue with him, but he cupped her face with his hands, silencing her protest. "I'm not going to let you stay in this house knowing he could come back. I'd never forgive myself if something happened to you."

She pulled away. "Reid, it's—"

"Just for one night." He took his hands away, remembering their agreement to keep things purely platonic. "I've got plenty of room. Tomorrow we'll decide what to do about arming this place with some security so I don't have to—" He cleared his throat. "So, *we* don't have to worry about your safety."

She went upstairs to throw a few things into her suitcase while he checked every window and door in the house to make sure they were locked. First thing tomorrow, he'd set up a camera pointing to her backyard and connect it to his phone. The next time that guy showed up, he'd know immediately—and so would the local police. He didn't want Richard Jeffers to get within spitting distance of Alana ever again without him present.

They locked up and walked over to his house. Alana insisted on bringing the dog with her. Reid didn't feel like dealing with the fireworks that were sure to erupt between her dog and Hannah's big orange tabby, but he didn't want Alana to change her mind, either, so he gave in and allowed Dusty to stay overnight with her. Simon, the cat, would have to deal with it.

"This is the bedroom Nate uses when he comes to stay," Reid said as he showed Alana to her accommodations for the evening. He flipped the light switch and small lamps on the twin nightstands cast a soft glow to the homey atmosphere. The room was furnished with a queen-sized bed, a large television mounted on the wall and a private bath.

Dusty began sniffing around the room, detecting the scent of their cat. Simon slipped out from underneath the bed and arched his back. He hissed and growled then ran from the room and disappeared down the stairs.

"You can use this for a luggage rack." Reid lifted her suitcase and placed it on top of a large antique trunk in one corner. "Nate always does."

Nate's Sports-Illustrated Swimsuit Edition magazine lay on the dresser. Annoyed, Reid snatched it and rolled it up, shoving it into his back pocket. "If you need anything, let me know."

She flashed a grin, revealing her amusement. "I'll be fine. I'm going to get into my jammies and spend the evening watching Hallmark movies." She tossed her purse on the bed. "I need a break."

"Sounds like a good plan."

He wanted to put his arms around her again and just hold her for a while to let her know how glad he was that she was safe, but because of their agreement, he simply said good night instead and walked out of her room, shutting the door behind him.

Chapter Nine

The next morning Alana awoke to a small voice whispering in her ear.

"Lana, are you sleeping?"

Even in the drowsy haze that clouded her brain, she couldn't help smiling to herself. "Not any more, Hannah."

"When are you going to get up?"

She yawned and pulled the thick, down comforter over her head. "I don't know. This bed is so comfortable I might stay here all day."

A pair of small hands pulled the comforter away from her face. "You haf to get up, Lana."

"Why?"

Hannah's clear blue eyes focused seriously on hers. "Because Dadee is making pana-cakes for you."

"He is?"

Hannah's blonde curls bounced as she nodded. "And bacon." Hannah eagerly helped pull the comforter all the way off of her.

Alana sat up and looked around. "Where's Dusty?"

Hannah pointed toward the doorway. "She had to go potty. Da-dee let her go outside." She let out an exaggerated sigh. "Simon don't like her. He scratched her nose."

"Okay, now you've convinced me. I'm getting up." Alana slipped out of bed and put on her thick, terry robe over her nightgown then shoved her feet into a pair of fluffy slippers. The pungent aroma of fresh coffee filled her nostrils. "That coffee smells so good. I'm seriously in need of a cup right now. Lead the way." She followed Hannah down to the kitchen.

Dusty sat under the table, watching Reid intently.

"Good morning," Reid said cheerily as he stood at the stove frying bacon. He wore a white T-shirt and a pair of navy and red plaid pajama bottoms. His thick, golden hair brushed the nape of his neck in unruly curls. "Did you sleep well?"

"Yes. That bed is really comfortable," Alana said as she headed toward the coffee pot. "I hated to leave it, but a little bird whispering in my ear told me someone was making breakfast."

"Nothing gets past that busy little bird." Reid laughed. "Nate told me he wouldn't stay over unless I bought a specific brand of mattress for him. It cost a small fortune." Bacon slices popped and sizzled in the frying pan as he turned them over with a long fork. It looked like a utensil for the grill. He looked up. "The mugs are in the cabinet above the pot. Pour me another cup, too."

Alana poured their coffee and sat down at the round kitchen table. "Let me know when you're ready and I'll set the table for breakfast."

"You just sit there and enjoy yourself," Reid said as he grabbed his steaming mug. "I've got this."

Hannah twirled around in her Tinkerbell pajamas. "I'll help, too!"

Reid placed crisp slices of bacon on thick paper towels covering a large cutting board and turned off the heat under the pan. "So, what are your plans for today?"

Alana sighed as she helped Hannah get into her booster seat. "You mean after I check my email for replies to my job applications? More packing and cleaning, I guess. I've finished the dining room and now I have to haul all of the boxes to storage. Why, did you have something else in mind? A new lead to investigate so I can put it off for one more day?"

He opened a cabinet and took out a couple plates. "You need a security system on the premises. I was thinking of getting some equipment today and setting it up. You're not safe any longer staying in that house by yourself."

Alana rested her chin on the palm of her hand. "This town is one place I never thought I'd feel unsafe. It makes me sad. My condo in downtown Minneapolis is more secure than the town of Merrick seems to be. If I can't feel protected in my grandmother's house, where can I go?" She looked up. "What has happened to this world?"

"I don't know," Reid said as he set the plates and silverware on the table. Reaching into the refrigerator, he pulled out a container of orange juice and set it on the table along with a pitcher of syrup and a plate of butter. "The principal reason I moved here was to get my daughter out of the city, but it's become evident that the issues I had with living in the city have followed me here."

He set two platters filled with the pancakes and bacon on the table and sat down. "Let's put this discussion on hold for now and enjoy our breakfast."

They passed the platters back and forth, piling their plates with food and were discussing the fact that Hannah would be starting school soon, when the door to the screen porch swung open.

"Knock, knock!" Jemma's clear voice rang out. "Good morning!"

Alana froze, her fork suspended in mid-air. Sitting at Reid's table in her bathrobe made her look as guilty as sin...

Hannah fed a piece of bacon to the dog.

"I hope you don't mind my coming over so early, Reid, but I bought some fresh kolacky on sale at the bakery and—"

Wearing a long, sweeping cape in dark green, Jemma stopped at the kitchen door and gasped, dropping the box of kolacky on the floor.

Alana dropped her fork. It clattered on the table.

Reid choked on his coffee.

Dusty pushed a kolacky with her nose and began to wolf it down.

For a moment, no one spoke as the shock of Jemma's untimely arrival sunk in.

"Well," Jemma said dramatically, her gaze scanning the scene, "I can clearly see what's going on here." She glared at Alana. "You just couldn't resist, could you?"

Reid pushed back his chair and sprang to his feet. "Jemma, please, it's not what you think."

Jemma laughed, though tears were already forming in her moss-colored eyes. "Don't insult me, Reid. It's exactly what I think. You two have been sneaking around together behind my back since the day you met." She pointed an accusing finger at Alana. "She told me all about it!"

Alana stood up. "Jemma, that's not true! We haven't done anything wrong; I swear!" Jemma whirled around to leave, but Alana rushed to her side. "Please, Jemma, don't leave. Let's talk this over. I can explain. Reid is right, the situation is *not* how it looks. Far from it."

Jemma stopped and gripped the door. "You just don't get it, do you?"

Alana blinked. "What do you mean?"

"I *mean*," Jemma said slowly, "you're so used to having it all that you just don't understand what it's like to be lonely and alone. To want for anything. You're beautiful and smart and self-confident. I've always been in awe of you—and I've always stood in your shadow watching you excel in everything you put your mind to do." Her voice trembled. "You can have any man you want, but I guess having *any* guy isn't as fun as taking mine away from me."

"Oh, Jemma," Alana said softly. "I didn't know you felt that way and I'm sorry if I've ever done anything to make you feel less than the most important person in the world to me. Please, sit down and I'll explain everything."

"There's nothing to explain except how we went from best friends to this…." Jemma shook her head. "I must be the world's biggest fool. Excuse me, but I have to go."

"No, don't leave because of me. You're not the biggest fool. I am," Alana said, her voice breaking. "I should never have agreed to stay on here while my parents went on their anniversary trip. Though I meant well, I've done nothing but cause trouble." She turned away and headed toward the stairway to the second floor, but stopped at the living room doorway and stared at Reid. "You don't need to bother with setting up a security system. I won't need it now. As soon as I change clothes, I'm leaving Merrick. And I'm never coming back."

"Alana, don't—"

She turned and ran through the house, nearly blinded by tears. She'd lost her grandmother, the house that gave her the best memories and now her closest friend. All because of a man. When would she ever learn?

***

Reid didn't know who to go after first. Through the window, he saw Jemma in the driveway and he charged out of the house after her. "Jemma, wait! Come back into the house and the three of us will talk this out."

She kept on going. "There isn't anything left to talk about," she replied, shouting the words over her shoulder. "Your actions speak loud and clear."

He caught up to her and grabbed her by the shoulders, gently spinning her around. "Look, Jemma, you and I need to come to an understanding. What I do in my own home is my business and I don't need to justify my actions to you or anyone else. Is that clear?" He dropped his arms and stepped back. "Alana stayed overnight because I was worried about her safety. We've uncovered some information about Essie's death and I was concerned about her staying alone. She slept in Nate's room. Not with me."

Jemma's eyes narrowed. "If you don't need to justify your actions to me, why bother with an explanation?"

"Because I respect you, Jemma, and I think of you as a good friend."

She looked downcast. "That's all I've ever been to you, isn't it?"

"Yes," he said gently. "There is no *us* and there never was. We had dinner once—by chance. Since then, you've stretched that evening completely out of proportion and the nature of our relationship, too. We're friends and that's all we've ever been. I've never given you any indication I wanted to be more. I've always been truthful with you about my feelings."

Her eyes filled with fresh tears, making him feel like the lowest man on earth. Perhaps he *was* the lowest man on earth for failing to do something about it a long time ago, but he had never wanted to hurt her. Perhaps if he had been firm with her right away, he wouldn't be breaking her heart now.

"A girl can dream, can't she?"

"Aw, Jemma," he said and slid his arm around her shoulder. "I'm sorry. I think the world of you and you know it. I'll always consider you a close friend and I'm truly glad you're Hannah's teacher this year. I can't imagine anyone better qualified to trust her with than you."

"I love her like she was my own." Jemma sniffed. "I wish I had a child like her."

"You will someday." Reid took her hands in his. "I promise. You're a beautiful woman, inside and out. You'll find the right man and the happiness you deserve."

She looked up. "Do you still want me to take care of Hannah when you go out of town?"

"Of course, I do." He smiled. "I'm counting on it."

After Jemma left, Reid went back into the kitchen and found Hannah eating her pancake as though nothing had happened. The dog, on the other hand, had gobbled every single kolacky in the box. All that remained of Jemma's treat were paper napkins scattered across the kitchen floor.

Alana appeared in the kitchen dragging her suitcase behind her.

"You don't have to do this," he argued. "Talk to Jemma. Don't allow a stupid misunderstanding to destroy a lifetime of friendship. I've made peace with her and you can do the same."

She stared at him as she rolled her suitcase through the kitchen. "It's too late. I've betrayed her trust and ruined our relationship forever."

"What about the investigation?"

"I just...I can't think about that right now. I'm too upset." She stopped in front of him. "I have no doubt you'll find a way to prove Richard Jeffers committed murder. When you do, I hope you get the credit you so richly deserve. Goodbye, Reid."

Wiping away tears, she walked out of his life.

Chapter Ten

Alana drove away from Grandma Essie's house and left the town of Merrick, distraught and in tears. She cried all the way back to Minneapolis. By the time she drove into the underground garage of her condominium tower, she'd worn herself out. She grabbed her bag, clutched Dusty by the collar and took the elevator to her place, hoping she didn't encounter anyone on the way. She didn't feel like explaining why her face looked like a tomato. Or why she had brought a stray dog with her to Minneapolis.

As soon as she dropped her bag in her condo, she took Dusty up to the rooftop for the dog to do her business in the pet relief area. She wasn't sure if it would work to keep a dog in a condo in the heart of downtown Minneapolis, but until she found a permanent home for Dusty, she didn't have any other choice.

Alana spent the next couple days resting and watching television with Dusty by her side. She was exhausted, both physically and emotionally and it felt good to simply lay around and do nothing for a change.

Her condo looked the same as she had left it, but something had changed. It no longer felt like home. Though the beautiful, spacious rooms were exquisitely decorated, they lacked the warmth and character of Grandma Essie's high ceilings, wide woodwork and wallpapered rooms. Her footsteps pattered on the marble tiles as she walked through the open kitchen. Their echo made the room sound like an empty shell. The truth was, it was missing the giggles and joyful exuberance of a little girl and the deep, rumble of her father's laughter. She missed the jingle of Jemma's bracelets and the woman's quick wit. She missed being with all of them every minute of every day.

After a week, Alana sat at her polished, cherrywood desk and penned a letter to Jemma, pouring out her heart. She'd spent days thinking about what she wanted to say and how she wanted to say it. Jemma deserved more than just a brief "I'm sorry" that morning at Reid's house.

Then she wrote one to Reid.

She shoved the stamped envelopes into the mail chute on her floor and felt a huge burden lift from her shoulders. She was ready to make peace with both of them, and she didn't know if either of them would take her words to heart, but it felt good to know she had done the right thing.

One morning a few days later, her phone awoke her. She'd been back for ten days now and hadn't told anyone she was home again so she'd had very few calls. She hadn't even visited her closest neighbor, Gina.

The phone rang again. She lifted her head and stuck the phone up to her ear. "Hello?"

"Hey, sleepyhead. It's Chad. How are you enjoying your paid vacation?" Chad Thompson, the product director of her old team at Dorale Systems was usually a happy guy, but today he sounded jollier than ever.

"Oh, ha-ha." She punched up her pillow and laid back down. "It would be a lot more fun if it was a better paying one. My last paycheck went so fast for bills I practically got whiplash watching the money fly out of my account. I'm waiting for my first unemployment check to come."

"How is your job search coming along?"

She yawned and rubbed her eyes with the heel of her free hand. "Well, I'm searching, but nothing has come along." Another loud yawn. "How about you? Did you find a job or are you still filling out apps and making regular trips to the food shelf?"

Chad laughed. "I thank God it's not that bad. My wife still has a job but now I've been demoted to Daddy Daycare and I'm getting desperate." He laughed again. "I don't know how women can do this all day. By the time my wife gets home, I'm ready for a couple Tylenol and an ice pack. And a six-pack of beer."

Alana couldn't help laughing and decided to forgive him for waking her from a sound sleep. "Is there a purpose to this call? Or are you just looking for sympathy?"

"Yeah, I've actually got some good news. I may have landed at job at Rockwell Corporation."

"O-h-h-h-h. That's good money." The Rockwell chain of stores nationwide were becoming major competitors to Target. Word on the street was they were expanding in every area to keep up with their phenomenal growth.

"Yeah," Chad replied enthusiastically. "They've narrowed down the field of candidates to me and one other. If I get it, I'll be putting together my own team. Are you interested?"

She sat up in bed, fully awake. "Are you kidding? Of course, I am! When do you expect them to make a decision?"

"Soon," he said vaguely. "But the team won't be hired until after the first of the year."

"Oh." She fell back on the pillow. It was only the sixth of September. The new year was a long way off...

"Hey, look at it this way. You'll get to enjoy the holidays with your family."

"Yeah, and wave bye-bye to my car when the tow truck pulls up to repossess it."

"Hang on, okay?" Chad said seriously. "Ask your parents for money if you have to. I'll try to get you on board as soon as possible."

"Okay." *Get the job first...*

She hung up feeling encouraged for the first time in weeks. It wasn't a sure thing, but it was the best news she'd had since Dorale shut its doors and left everyone to join the unemployment line.

***

Alana had just finished scrubbing the shower in her bathroom when her phone rang. She'd had to cancel the services of her cleaning woman indefinitely and start doing household chores herself, but the lady had been gracious enough to leave her with a few products to get her started.

Cleaning was hard work! She'd gained a new appreciation of what it took to do the job and vowed to give her cleaning lady a raise when she could afford to hire the woman back.

The phone rang again. Blowing a few stray hairs from her face, she located her phone on the kitchen counter and looked at the screen. It was the security guard's office on the main floor.

She shed her rubber gloves and answered the call on speakerphone. "This is Alana Morgan."

"This is the security desk," a deep male voice said. "There's a package down here that the Fed Ex delivery person says you need to sign for."

"Oh…" She hesitated, puzzled. What in the world was that all about? She hadn't purchased anything online since she lost her job. Besides, it was Labor Day. She had no idea Fed Ex delivered on a holiday. "I'll be right down."

She cringed, hoping it wasn't a registered letter from a bill collector or something equally as dire. But then…maybe it was a fun gift from her parents! They would be running around England by now, seeing as much as they could before catching their multi-country tour that started in London and ended in Rome, Italy. Excited about the possibility of receiving something unique from Britain, she grabbed her phone and left her condo.

The elevator doors whisked open when she reached the main floor. She hurried across the lobby to the security guard's office preoccupied with the contents of the package when three people literally stepped out in front of her.

"Surprise!"

Reid, Hannah and Jemma stood in the lobby, smiling. So, this was her surprise package?

Oh…my…gosh…

Her mouth gaped in astonishment. "Jemma…Reid…Hannah! What…what are you doing here?"

Reid laughed as he set Hannah on the floor. His blond curls were as unruly as ever. His eyes had never been so blue or twinkled as much as they did now. "We've come to check out your cool digs then take you out for dinner." He took her hands in his. "We've missed you."

"Hi, Lana," Hannah said, her round face beaming. "Do you haf cookies at your house?"

Alana bent down and kissed the top of Hannah's curly head. "Why, yes, I do!"

"We received your letters," Jemma said softly. Her eyes were shining with emotion. She didn't say anything more, but Alana understood. They wanted to talk to her privately.

"Come with me." Alana took Hannah by the hand. "Let's go up to my place and see Dusty. She's waiting for you!"

Hannah marched along asking questions about everything she saw. Alana tried to give her simple answers, but that only prompted more questions.

"It's her new thing," Reid said with a sigh as they entered the elevator. "We play twenty questions, then we play twenty more."

When they arrived at Alana's floor, she unlocked the door with her phone and ushered them into her condo. Dusty met them in the entryway, jumping for joy and wagging her tail. Hannah laughed and tried to pet the dog, but Dusty wouldn't settle down.

After a tour of the condo and a round of cold beverages, everyone got comfortable in the living room. Everyone except Hannah. She became enamored with the prospect of looking at everything and touching everything she saw.

"Why don't you have another cookie," Alana suggested and exchanged an Oreo for a small Murano glass figurine—a Millefiori cat sculpture. She spread a blanket on the white leather sofa and set Hannah on it, sticky fingers and all.

"So, you got my letters," Alana said tentatively. "I meant every word I wrote and I still do." She stared into her crystal wine glass then looked up. "I should have used better judgment with you both and considered your feelings."

She looked at Jemma. "I didn't mean to cause a rift between you and Reid. Knowing how you felt about him at the time, it was selfish of me to make friends with him behind your back and plan out Grandma Essie's investigation without involving you."

She glanced at Reid. "She knows, right?"

He nodded. "I told her everything."

Jemma shook her head at Alana, her long curls bouncing about her shoulders. "No, it wasn't selfish at all. You were just being you. I shouldn't have been so judgmental." She grabbed Alana's hand and twined their fingers together. "Reid and I had several long talks about your letters and he convinced me to accompany him on this trip to see you." She squeezed Alana's hand; tears glistening in her eyes. "You and I are both only children and we've been like siblings all of our lives. I couldn't stay mad at my only sister."

Alana leaned over and hugged her best friend with all her might. "I couldn't, either," she whispered. "I'm so glad you're here."

They sat and talked for an hour, catching up on all the latest gossip in Merrick and all of the preparations Jemma had been doing in her classroom in anticipation of her new class that was starting tomorrow.

Reid was noticeably quiet. He stood and walked over to the open drapes, gazing out the floor-to-ceiling window at the city skyline.

Jemma excused herself to visit the restroom, leaving Alana and Reid alone.

Hannah had fallen asleep on the sofa.

Reid took her hand and squeezed it. The strength of his palm curling around hers gave her pulse a rush.

"She was miserable without you," he said quietly. "Nothing would cheer her up. Then we both got your letters and I made a decision." He leaned close. "One way or the other, you two were going to make up. I was determined to see you two become friends again." He grinned. "I really didn't expect it to be this easy, though."

"I'll always be grateful to you for doing this," Alana said from the bottom of her heart. "Are you and Jemma...you know...together now?"

"Just friends." Reid shrugged. "That's all we were ever meant to be and now that we have our boundaries established our relationship is better than ever."

They sat in silence for a few moments then he looked deeply into her eyes. Her heart began to flutter erratically. She suddenly knew what he was about to say…

He took both of her hands in his. "I've missed you, Alana. Hannah and I both have. She asks about you every day." His long fingers intertwined with hers. "I think about you every *moment* of the day. I used to think I didn't need anyone else in my life, but I'm lost without you."

"Oh Reid…" She could barely speak over the racing of her heart. "I've—I've missed you, too—"

Jemma rejoined them. "Well, did you ask her?"

Alana glanced from Jemma to Reid, puzzled. "Ask me what?"

Reid gave her a solemn look. "Come back to Merrick with us, Alana. I've shared with Jemma everything you and I discovered about Essie's death. She's agreed to step in and help with the investigation, but we're missing a vital member of the team—*you*. Come back and help us uncover the truth."

Jemma nodded in agreement. "Besides," she added, "Reid says the roofers are going to start working in a couple days and another team is supposed to show up at the end of the week to raise the front porch. And then the painters are coming. You need to be there to give final approval and pay the bills."

Their words were like processed sugar in her veins. Filled with new enthusiasm and renewed purpose, Alana sprang from the sofa. "I'll just go throw a few things into my suitcase." She hurried into the bedroom and opened the mirrored door to her walk-in closet. She pulled leggings, sweaters and tops off their hangers and dumped them into her large blue travel bag.

Oh, and I need shoes, too, she thought happily. *Must have shoes!*

She scooped up an armful of running shoes, spiked heels, fashion boots and everything in between, dumping them on top of the clothes. Snapping her fingers, she ran into the bathroom to load up on toiletries. "Where are we going to dinner? I feel like I haven't eaten for days!"

Truthfully, she hadn't had much of an appetite lately. She'd been bored and depressed. Worried about the future.

Not today, though, she thought excitedly. *I'm going back to Merrick.*

***

Reid walked Alana to the back door of Essie's house and carried her suitcase up the stairs, waiting while she deactivated the alarm. Hannah was sound asleep in the car so he couldn't stay long, but what he needed to say he hoped would last a lifetime.

He set her suitcase down next to the door. "Hey," he said softly as he placed his hand on her elbow and gently turned her around. "This is the first chance I've had all day to get you all to myself and I'm going to make the most of it." Her face brightened as he slid his arms around her waist and pulled her close. "I'm so glad you've come back. This is where you belong, Alana."

She circled her arms around his neck and gazed into his eyes. "I used to love the fast pace of living in downtown Minneapolis but once I went back, I realized how much I missed this little town—and Jemma. Most of all, I missed you and Hannah."

He angled his head and brushed her lips, tentatively at first, to gauge her reception, but when she raised up on her toes and tightened her arms around his neck, he gave himself fully to the kiss. He wanted her to know how he felt about her in more than just words.

He pulled her closer and kissed her again, intoxicated by the softness of her lips, the sweet aroma of her hair. "I've wanted to do this ever since I saw you this morning," he whispered in her ear, "but I didn't know how you'd feel about it. After the last time I tried—"

"I was convinced that kissing you would be betraying my best friend." She let out a deep sigh. "Even though I knew you didn't have any romantic feelings for her. Not only that, but I'd just ended a bad relationship and I was convinced that all I needed in my life right now was my career."

He caressed her cheek with his thumb. "What changed your mind?"

"Seeing you again...I realized just how truly lonely I'd been without you."

He silenced her with a passionate kiss.

A muffled wail echoed from the car.

Reid reluctantly pulled away. "Sounds like Hannah's awake. I'd better go. She's had a long day today and she's got her first day of school tomorrow. I need to bathe her and get her into bed early..." He placed his finger under Alana's chin and kissed her goodbye.

"See you tomorrow." Alana said with an understanding nod. She held up one hand and waved goodbye as he slowly backed away.

He headed for his SUV in the driveway, happier than he'd been in a long time.

***

Reid carried Hannah's backpack as he escorted her into Merrick Elementary for her first day of school. The brick, one-story building buzzed like a beehive with happy kids, scurrying to their classrooms to meet their new teachers and reconnect with friends they hadn't seen since the final day of school early last June.

Reid had previously visited this building last week with Jemma to check out Hannah's classroom and learn the layout of the school. He had to drop Hannah off every morning and pick her up every afternoon and wanted to be sure he was on time the first day.

Hannah walked beside him in her new pink dress with a black kitty on the front and white leggings underneath, chattering as usual. Her black, patent leather shoes had bows fastened on the front. He'd brushed her hair to a soft sheen and bound it with an elastic band into a long curly ponytail. It didn't appear to bother her that he was about to leave her in a strange place with a group of noisy, unruly children. They made their way down a wide, busy hallway with cinderblock walls painted in pastel colors and polished floors. On the wall, a large sign read "Welcome Students."

Reid found Hannah's kindergarten classroom and escorted her inside. Jemma stood off to one side, holding a large box of tissues and consoling a distraught mother who was apparently having separation issues with her child. He glanced around. About twenty children were clustered at the other end of the room, laughing and playing with puzzles, large alphabet blocks and other brightly-colored toys. Some sat on tiny chairs at knee-high tables, coloring on white sheets of paper.

Hannah stood at his side, wide-eyed, watching the children with interest.

He bent down on one knee. "Daddy has to leave you now, honey, but I'll be back this afternoon to pick you up." He straightened the rounded collar on her dress. "You're going to have a fun first day getting to know all of your new classmates. Jemma is here, too."

Hannah didn't hear a word he said. Her bright blue eyes were focused on the activity going on at the opposite end of the room. He let go of her collar and she began to walk toward her new classmates, slowly at first, but the closer she got to the swarm of happy kids, the faster she moved.

Reid stood and watched her join the group. A tight, painful knot suddenly formed in the middle of his throat.

Bye, honey.

He swallowed hard and made his way to the door, but turned around to make sure Hannah was adjusting to his departure.

She was so busy playing with her new friends, she'd forgotten all about him.

Jemma gave him an understanding smile and signaled to leave the backpack on the floor with the others then went back to her conversation.

He walked out of the school feeling greatly relieved that Hannah hadn't cried when he left, but at the same time, the situation had left *him* unexpectedly downcast. His little girl was growing up. She was no longer the laughing, chubby baby he used to bounce on his knee or rock back to sleep in the middle of the night. Those days were gone forever. Today started a new chapter in their lives.

He passed the lunchroom and the aroma of something baking filled his nostrils, making him hungry. He glanced in. Across the room, a dark-haired woman was busy setting up equipment on a table. Though she looked older and wore black-framed glasses, the woman reminded him of Monique.

He shook his head and walked on. He hadn't heard a peep out of his ex-wife since she'd called him on his private line three weeks ago and threatened him. She must have been bluffing.

Good, he thought angrily. The last thing Hannah needed was to have her mother turn her life upside down. The child was happy and well-balanced. She deserved to stay that way

.

Chapter Eleven

Roofers were shooting staples into shingles on the roof. A cement crew had raised the porch with temporary jacks and were pouring footings underneath it. The Koktavy and Daleiden painting crew had fixed the water damage in the upstairs bedroom and were currently painting all the ceilings in the house. The new stone countertops and appliances were scheduled to be delivered tomorrow.

Alana didn't know what to do with herself. She felt out of place in the midst of so much activity going on around her. In her personal realm, Reid was frantically working on his newest book on excellence in leadership, Jemma was at school teaching her class, and all of her other girlfriends were busy with their jobs. She, on the other hand, didn't have a thing to do except wander around and watch everyone else.

She'd been back in Merrick for two weeks now, anxious to get the house repairs underway, but everything had gotten off to a slow start. Due to off and on periods of prolonged rain, the roofing project had been delayed several times. The cement contractors failed to show up when they had promised and the appliances had been backordered for weeks.

There was one silver lining—the delays had given Alana time to finish completely cleaning out the house and garage. The storage unit, however, could not hold one more box. As it was, she could barely get the door shut. She still had all of Grandma Essie's Christmas decorations in the storage compartments under the eaves, including the tree, but didn't have the heart to take them to the thrift store.

Her phone rang. It was Reid. "Hey, what's up?"

"I need a big favor." He sounded frazzled.

"Sure. What do you want me to do?"

"I'm supposed to pick up Hannah in five minutes, but I'm running seriously behind. Could you run up to her school and get her? Your name is on the list of people allowed to pick her up. I'll call the office right now to let them know you're coming."

Are you kidding me? Gladly...

"No problem," she said. "I'll leave right away."

He let out a sigh of relief. "Thanks. I owe you."

Reid was due to leave for his leadership conference in Chicago in a few days and she knew he had a million things to do. She'd offered to keep Hannah for him while he was gone, but Jemma always took care of Hannah now when he went out of town. She'd taken over Grandma Essie's job.

Alana hung up, grabbed her purse and ran outdoors to Grandma Essie's Roadmaster. She slid in and jammed the keys into the ignition. Wait a minute. Hannah needed her car seat. She jumped out of the car and headed over to Reid's house. He stood at the door holding the keys to his Pacifica. He tossed them to her.

"Thanks!" She took his car and made it to the school right on time.

A horde of chattering kids and parents streamed out the front doors. Alana waded against the dense tide of bodies and made her way into the school. After checking in at the office, she walked to the kindergarten classroom where Hannah was with Jemma, waiting for her.

Hannah waved. "Hi, Lana!"

"Hey, you're coming with me today. Is that okay?"

Hannah nodded vigorously. "Can I haf a cookie when we get home?"

"Of course!"

Alana had a brief chat with Jemma then grabbed Hannah's backpack and said goodbye.

They made their way out of the school. "Now, take my hand," Alana said as they stepped off the curb to cross the parking lot. "We need to watch for oncoming cars. This is a busy place."

"Oh-kay," Hannah said happily. She suddenly stopped. "Look, Lana! There's Monica!"

Preoccupied with traffic, Alana cast a quick glance in the direction Hannah pointed—and did a double take. A tall, dark-haired woman stood next to a black Silverado with chrome trim and dark-tinted windows, searching her purse for something.

Alana stopped and bent down, meeting Hannah face to face. "Who did you say that was?"

Hannah, waved, but the woman was busy getting into the pickup and didn't see her. "Monica."

"Who is Monica and how do you know her?"

Hannah squinted in the bright sunlight. "Oh, she makes lunch."

Oh-oh.

Warning bells suddenly went off in Alana's head. She turned around. "Come on, sweetie. We're going back into the school to see

Jemma for a minute, okay?"

Hannah nodded. "Oh-kay."

Alana gripped Hannah's hand and walked her back into the school.

Jemma was putting away sheets of colored construction paper and scissors when they returned to the classroom. The deepening of her brows indicated she immediately sensed a problem. "What's wrong?" She frowned at Hannah's backpack in Alana's hand. "Did I forget to pack something?"

Alana drew in a deep breath. "Who is Monica?"

"Monica Blake?" Jemma smiled, visibly relieved. "She's new. She works in the lunchroom."

"Do you know her very well?"

"Oh, yeah." Jemma set down the paper. "I met her last summer on the day of the kindergarten roundup event. The school had an all-staff meeting with a brunch in the morning. She sat at my table and we got to talking right away. We've been friends ever since. I talk to her practically every day. Why do you ask?"

"Hannah pointed her out to me in the parking lot and I got a little worried about her talking to strangers, that's all."

Alana said goodbye to Jemma again and called Reid as soon as she got Hannah strapped into her car seat. "Hannah's fine and we're on our way home, but there's something I need to tell you."

A pregnant pause…

"I just saw the black Silverado in the parking lot. According to Jemma, the woman who drives it is called Monica Blake and she works here at the school. And Hannah is on a first-name basis with her."

Alana took the phone away from her ear and covered it with her hand. She didn't want Hannah to hear her father swearing at the top of his lungs.

***

Reid paced the floor, trying to walk off some steam, but it was turning out to be a futile exercise. Nothing would calm him down until he got to the bottom of this issue with *Monica Blake*. He was nervous, anxious and angry at the same time and the more he thought about her, the worse he became. Did she really think she could get away with this ridiculous deception? Her last name was a dead giveaway. It was her maiden name.

No wonder I haven't heard from Monique. She's been here all along. Right under my nose. Talking to Hannah every day, sneaking her way back into the kid's life.

He heard his car pull slowly into the driveway. Alana hadn't even come to a full stop before he'd reached the back steps, taking two at a time. He walked toward the car and waited for her to shut it off so he could open the door and pull Hannah out of her seat—and into his arms.

Alana shut off the car and got out. "Let's go inside. I don't feel comfortable discussing things out here." She grabbed her purse and followed him as he carried Hannah into the house.

Reid set Hannah in her booster chair with a juice box and grabbed an apple out of the refrigerator.

Alana set her purse on the table. "There's something about this woman you're not telling me."

"There's a *lot* I haven't told you." Reid washed the apple then grabbed a steak knife and began to cut it into thin slices.

"Well…" She sat down at the table. "There's no time like the present."

"Let me get Hannah squared away and then we'll talk." Reid finished his work then set Hannah in front of the TV in the living room to watch her favorite kid's show with the juice box, a couple apple slices and a few cheese crackers in a bowl.

He walked back into the kitchen and grabbed himself a bottle of beer from the refrigerator. "Want one?"

At her nod, he grabbed a second one and twisted the caps off both of them. Then he sat down and let out a tense breath. "I actually saw her the other day. She doesn't look like I remember her so I didn't recognize her." He took a swig of beer. "She looks older, wears glasses now and she's changed her hair."

Alana stared at him, a knowing look on her face. "Your ex-wife."

He exhaled another tense breath. "Her real name is Monique." He drummed his fingers on the table, thinking furiously about what this new information meant. "You're sure she was the one driving the Silverado?"

"I saw her get into the driver's seat."

Reid clutched his beer. "You know what this means, don't you?"

"Yeah, she's in a relationship with Richard Jeffers." Alana's brows lifted. "She got the job at the school to be close to her daughter without you knowing about it."

Reid closed his eyes. "Jeffers wants to buy the house next door to me so Monique can move in and see her daughter every day—"

"—but the old lady wouldn't sell, wouldn't have anything to do with him," Alana said, interrupting him. "So, he pushed her off the back steps, thinking that once she was out of the way, the family would put it up for sale and he'd make them an offer they couldn't refuse."

They were silent for a moment.

Reid studied her. "Are you thinking the same thing I am?"

Alana set down her beer. "What if the family won't sell? What will he do, kill them all?"

"No, probably not," Reid replied. "That would be too drastic, but he'll come up with something. Burn the house down and buy the land or break into it and trash the place… Something ominous to wear down your parents." He slammed his beer on the table. "We have to stop him before this goes any farther."

Alana went silent and picked at the label on her bottle.

"What?"

"Monique made friends with Jemma last summer and I think she's been pumping Jemma for information without Jemma's knowledge." She pealed a thin slice of paper off the bottle. "It's none of my business," Alana said cautiously, "but what's the story with your ex-wife? Why did you divorce her?"

Reid stood up. He hadn't told anyone this story except Nate and his lawyer. Not even his parents. "After Hannah was born, Monique went through a rough patch with depression. She was really down so I thought I'd take her away for a week. I figured she could take in some new scenery and just have fun. I was the CEO of an auto parts corporation at the time and we were sponsoring a vehicle at NASCAR, so I took her to see the race."

He leaned against the counter and stared down at his beer. "She had a great time and after we got home, she seemed to improve a lot." He took a swig of beer and set it on the table. He'd suddenly lost his desire for it. "One day I came home from work early as a surprise to take her and the baby to lunch. Hannah was sleeping in her crib, but Monique wasn't in the apartment. I thought maybe she'd stepped out to visit with a neighbor, but after fifteen minutes passed, I started getting worried. She shouldn't have left Hannah alone that long. Another ninety minutes went by before she finally showed up."

Alana watched him intently and he had the feeling she knew the end of the story.

"She made some excuse that she'd been exercising and lost track of the time, but I could tell she was lying. So, I came home at the same time the next day and Hannah was in her bed, but Monique was gone again. I picked up the baby and went down to the security guard's office. The security guard confirmed that during the week, Monique left every day at eleven and came back at one. And she'd been doing it for several months, ever since we came back from NASCAR. She'd met someone there who'd followed her back to Minneapolis and she was seeing him every day."

"Good grief. How could she do that to her own child?" Alana rolled her eyes in disgust. "What did you do then?"

Reid dumped his beer in the sink. "I got copies of all the security videos and filed for divorce. I gave her the lion's share of our net worth in exchange for her parental rights. Then I quit my job, left town and reinvented myself." He tossed the bottle into the recycling bin. "She got millions out of me. I don't know how much is left but she's probably still wealthy. That's why Jeffers is driving a hundred-thousand-dollar truck."

Alana stood up. "And wearing a gold Cartier watch, diamonds, designer perfume and offering ten percent above market rate for a rundown house with cash. He'll do anything to keep her happy so he can keep spending her money." She grabbed her purse. "What are you going to do about her?"

"I think it's time to shake things up a bit," Reid said as he folded his arms. "Tomorrow, I'm going to blow her cover."

***

After he put Hannah to bed, Reid called Nate.

"Yeah," Nate said in his usual gruff tone of voice.

"How tied up are you at the moment? I need a favor."

"Why." Nate sounded preoccupied, like he always did.

"I need to film a confession."

"For what."

Reid wished he could see Nate's face. "A murder."

The crashing sound when Nate's phone hit the floor made Reid pull his phone away from his ear—with a chuckle.

"Aren't you a little busy to be getting mixed up in a local theater production? You're due in Chicago next Tuesday," Nate said once he came back on the line.

"This isn't a theater production," Reid said, irritated. "This is *for real*." He waited while Nate processed the information then he proceeded to describe in detail what he needed the equipment for. "I want it all down here by tomorrow afternoon."

"I can have it there by tonight."

"Great. I'll see you in a couple hours."

Chapter Twelve

The next morning, Alana looked out her kitchen window and saw a strange vehicle in Reid's driveway. It looked like a vintage Volkswagen bus, the kind she'd seen in old movies. In avocado green, no less. She was surprised it didn't have those weird psychedelic flowers plastered all over it. A middle-aged man wearing jeans, cowboy boots, a black T-shirt and a wrinkled linen blazer stood pulling boxes of wires and equipment out of it. His brown hair was parted in the middle and pulled back into a man-bun in the back of his head. She gawked at him through the window.

Who is that?

Curious, she turned off the new alarm system on the house and walked over to Reid's place to check out his visitor. Back in Minneapolis, she would have never approached a strange man in the parking garage at her condo tower, but this was Merrick and the man stood in Reid's yard. The Merrick thing to do was to be neighborly. The man stopped what he was doing when he saw her coming through the gate.

"Hello. I'm Alana Morgan, Reid's neighbor."

The man nodded as he hoisted a large box from the van. "Nate

Gilbertson. I'm pleased to meet you."

Alana's smile froze on her face as she stared at him, stunned. This was *Nate*? The professor/agent Reid talked about incessantly? He didn't look at all like she'd envisioned. She pictured a tall, slim man with white hair and a close-cropped beard who wore a designer suit every day. A man who drove a large luxury car that always looked as impeccable as he kept his own appearance.

Reid appeared in the doorway of the screen porch. "Alana, have you met Nate?"

"Yes," she replied curiously, "just a moment ago." She watched Nate set the box on the ground and go back to the van for another one. "What's going on?"

Reid bounced down the steps and met her at the van. "We're setting up a surveillance system."

She squinted at him. "You're doing *what*?"

Reid looked around, as though worried someone might overhear him. "Come on inside and we'll talk."

Alana followed him into his kitchen and waited for his explanation.

"Nate is going to set up a camera system in your house to catch the confession of Jeffers on tape. We'll get him to own up to Essie's murder then turn the tape over to the police."

She blinked, dazed at the magnitude of what she'd just heard. "How are you going to pull that off?"

Reid grabbed a powdered doughnut out of a box and took a bite. "We're going set a trap with bait that he can't resist," he said with a mouth full of doughnut.

"You've got powdered sugar all over your face." Alana chuckled as she grabbed one out of the box. "Where did you get these, anyway?"

"They belong to Nate. It's his favorite junk food."

They went back outside and Alana began helping pull the equipment out of the van. They spent all day untangling wires, sorting out all of the items they needed then setting up the cameras and the recording equipment. They had just finished when Reid announced he had to go to Hannah's school.

"Just to let you know, I'm not going there to get Hannah. Jemma's bringing Hannah home," he said to Alana. "I don't want my daughter anywhere near that school when I approach Monique." He pulled out his keys. "It's not going to be pretty."

Alana placed her hand on his arm. "Be careful, okay? This could start a firestorm."

He reached out and brushed her cheek with his thumb. "I hope it does."

***

Reid drove his car through the front parking lot and went around to the west side of the school where the employees parked. He saw the Silverado sitting in the back row and pulled up next to it facing the opposite way so the driver's side of both vehicles were situated side by side. Within minutes, Monique emerged from the back door of the school, walking toward her hundred-thousand-dollar chariot.

Doesn't anybody around here think it's a bit rich for a lunch lady to be driving one of these?

The closer she came to the pickup, the more he could see how he could have mistaken her for someone else. She wore a drab uniform of light brown and had her hair cut short in a style he'd never seen her wear before. The most notable change, however, were her glasses. She'd ditched her contact lenses for the black plastic frames that dominated her face.

A deliberate disguise to keep her identity secret...

Unsuspecting, she walked straight toward him. He waited until she'd reached the vehicle before he lowered the window of his SUV.

"Hello, Monique."

She froze, staring at him in surprise.

"Oh," she said at last. "It's you. I didn't recognize you at first. You look different."

"So do you."

She looked offended by his remark and turned away as she pressed the unlocking device on her key fob. "What do you want." The sentence came out sounding more like a statement of indifference than a query.

"That's my question for you. What do *you* want?" *As if I didn't know...*

She opened the truck door then turned around, barely concealing her disdain. "You know what I want and I'll do whatever I have to do to get it."

He forced himself to remain calm. "So will I. It's called a restraining order and I can have one delivered to you quicker than a blink of an eye."

She glared at him. "Look, Reid, all I want is what's best for my daughter."

"Then leave town and never bother us again."

"Why should I? A little girl needs her mother."

He opened his vehicle door and slid out. "Hannah doesn't need a mother like you. She's happy and well-adjusted and I want her to remain that way." He pointed a finger in her face. "You stay away from her. Do you understand me?"

"You can't stop me from talking to her at school."

"I can hire a private investigator to look into the background of that dude you're shacking up with and hand the report over to the administrator. I'll bet they'll be plenty interested when they find out what kind of associations you have. The cops in this town might appreciate the information as well."

A muscle twitched in her cheek. "Rick has made some mistakes in the past, but he's turned his life around. He's a changed man."

That's the oldest excuse in the book. Don't make me laugh...

It didn't take a genius to figure out that Jeffers had a record and therefore the Silverado was in Monique's name.

"I don't care if *Rick* has had a brain transplant," Reid shouted. "He's not getting within a continent of my kid. And neither are you!"

Reaching up and clutching the grab handle in the truck, she pulled herself into the cabin and slammed the door. He watched, seething, as she tore out of the parking lot. He meant what he said—he'd go to any length to keep Hannah safe.

If this confrontation had started a war, it was about to go nuclear.

Chapter Thirteen

Alana stared at the wrinkled card as she stood in Reid's kitchen with him and Nate and dialed the cell phone number to Richard Jeffers. The phone went straight to voicemail. She listened to his message and waited for the beep. "Mr. Jeffers, this is Alana Morgan. I've changed my mind about the house. I've decided I want to sell it to you at ten percent over the market price before my parents get back from vacation. But I want to keep the ten percent amount as a private transaction between us, okay? In cash, as you suggested yesterday. Please call me at your earliest convenience."

She pressed the end button on her phone and set it on the table. "Do you think I sounded convincing?"

Reid smiled. "You sounded very…feminine. Just what appeals to Rick Jeffers, I'm sure."

"Rick? Is that what he goes by?"

"That's what Monique called him."

Alana stared at her phone. "He's creepy no matter what he calls himself."

Nate stared out the kitchen window. "Who is that?"

Alana immediately rushed to the window, wondering if Rick Jeffers had simply decided to show up again without calling, but it wasn't him.

Jemma stood on the back steps of Grandma Essie's house with Hannah, wearing a fawn-colored dress with a peasant blouse top and an ankle-length tiered skirt. Her arms and neck were laden with her favorite beads and bracelets. A fringed, burgundy shawl hugged her shoulders. She'd covered the crown of her thick coppery curls with a burgundy silk scarf and tied it at the nape so the sashes hung down her back.

"That's Jemma Bakken," Reid said, standing behind Alana. "I told her to meet us at Essie's place with Hannah."

"Nice Halloween costume," Nate said.

"That's no costume," Reid stated matter-of-factly. "That's how she always dresses."

"You don't say." Nate stared hard, as though spellbound. "Who is she?"

"She's Hannah's kindergarten teacher," Reid said, "and a good friend."

Nate gave him a sideways glance. "How good?"

"We're not romantically involved, if that's what you want to know."

Nate stared out the window again, fixated on Jemma. "Is she married? In a relationship?"

"No." Reid frowned. "What's with the third degree?"

Nate couldn't seem to pull his gaze away from the window. "How would you like to introduce me to her?"

Alana and Reid stared at each other in shock. Then they smiled.

"Sure," Alana said. "Let's go."

They met Jemma at the gate with Hannah. Jemma curiously studied Nate as they approached.

"Hi, I'm Nate Gilbertson," Nate said, not waiting for Alana or Reid to introduce him.

Jemma's eyes lit up like Christmas trees. "I'm Jemma Bakken," she said with a flirtatious lilt in her voice. "You must be Reid's editor."

"I'm his business partner," Nate replied, correcting her, though he was smiling. He held out his hand to shake.

"I'm pleased to meet you." Jemma extended her hand, her lips curving in a mischievous smile.

The moment the pair shook hands, Alana sensed invisible sparks glancing off them with such intensity that if they'd been standing close to power lines it would have caused a major outage.

Well, well, well... This should be interesting.

Jemma pointed to Nate's avocado green van. "I was wondering who owned that hippie wagon."

Nate blinked, looking as though he wasn't accustomed to women being so frank with him. "That's a *vintage* 1979 Volkswagen with a pop-up top."

She stared at it approvingly. "And it's *cherry*, too. It makes me think of Jimmy Hendrix."

Nate's eyes widened. "You're a Hendrix fan?"

"Of course." Jemma sashayed past him, swishing her skirt like a peacock spreading its tail.

Nate followed her to the van and slid open the side door to show her the interior.

Reid poked Alana with his elbow. "*Who knew?*" He leaned close.

"Geez, if I'd known they would hit it off this easily, I'd have introduced them a long time ago."

The group eventually settled in Reid's screen porch with a bottle of wine; sparkling, of course. And dry as a bone. Nate never drank anything else.

"This has a wonderful aroma," Jemma declared, swirling the wine in her flute. Her eyes sparkled more than the liquid.

Nate's gaze melted into hers. "Not as wonderful as you, I'm sure..."

Alana exchanged a look with Reid, letting him know it was time to get down to business.

Reid promptly brought up the subject of the recording equipment and Nate cut him off, filling Jemma in on the latest developments with Rick Jeffers. They all touched their glasses together in a toast to a successful endeavor.

Alana took a sip and the wine caught in her throat. Her eyes began to water as she swallowed it down and fought the urge to cough. She set the flute on the table and tried to focus.

Her phone rang.

Everyone went silent. Except Hannah.

"I wanna answer the phone." Hannah pulled on Alana's arm. "Can I? Pweeese?"

Alana looked at Jemma and cocked her head toward the back door.

"Off we go," Jemma said quickly to Hannah. "Let's go find Dusty." She whisked the child into her arms and carried her out of sight.

Alana cleared her throat and put the phone on speakerphone. "Hello?"

"Yeah, it's Jeffers. So, you want to sell now? You told me you didn't have the authority to do that."

"My parents didn't tell me to sell the house while they were gone, but they did give me a power of attorney to handle business in their absence so I guess that means I can do whatever I want, right?" She suggested a figure she wanted for the house, one that she and Reid had discussed prior to her phone message.

"Right. When can we meet?"

"I'll need to get the purchase agreement set up—"

"My attorney will handle that," Rick said. "I'll instruct him to keep the ten percent overpayment out of it. We'll do that transaction on the side. I'll have it ready by tomorrow."

Alana looked at Reid. "Great! Shall we say five o'clock?"

"I'll be there."

Rick Jeffers hung up.

Alana nervously looked at the men. "I guess we're on."

***

The next afternoon, Reid walked into Jemma's classroom at four o'clock. He wanted to personally deliver Hannah and Jemma to the Bakken family home—where they would also meet up with Alana—to make sure they were all safe and secure long before Rick Jeffers showed up at Alana's house. Nate had exchanged phone numbers with Alana and Jemma the day before and was already stationed in Essie's garage tweaking his equipment. Reid couldn't relax until he got these girls squared away so he could go back to Essie's house to wait for Jeffers to show up.

He walked into Jemma's classroom and found himself in the middle of kindergarten pandemonium. Students and parents milled about the room, locating backpacks, sweaters and hoodies before they headed home. Jemma was busy tying a little boy's shoe. "Where's Hannah?"

She gestured toward a table in the corner with her left hand. "She's right—" she whirled around; her face stricken. "Reid, she was right here a moment ago."

He knew something wasn't right, but he didn't want to frighten Jemma any more than she already was. She ran out into the hallway, calling for Hannah while Reid looked around the classroom in case his daughter might be hiding somewhere.

Jemma raced back into the room. "Reid! I can't find her." She put her hands over her face. "Oh, dear, where did she go?"

Sweat began to form on his upper lip. Panicking he said, "You check this room again. I'll check the rest of the school. She has to be here somewhere."

He raced from room to room in the school, maneuvering his way through the people in the hallway. After ten minutes, he ended back at Jemma's room. Mr. Wainright, the principal, was with her, looking grave as Jemma cried unconsolably. Her classroom stood empty now.

"We'll need to inform the police," the elderly man said. He pulled his phone from his pocket.

"Wait, I've got an idea I'd like to try first," Reid said hastily. He turned to Jemma. "Call your friend Monica."

Jemma looked up through a wad of tissue. "Why?"

"Did you talk to her today?"

"Yes, she stopped by a few minutes ago." Jemma sobbed. "We only visited for a moment. She said she'd call me later."

"Did you see her leave?"

Jemma shook her head. "I was busy getting my kids out the door. What would Monica know about Hannah's disappearance?"

"It's just a hunch. Dial her number and I'll talk to her." Reid squeezed her shoulder. *"Do it now, Jemma."*

She fished her phone from her purse and made the call. Monique answered on the second ring. Jemma held out the phone so everyone could hear.

"Jemma, darling! I don't have time to talk. I'm a little tied up right now. Can I call you back later?" Monique spoke in that sickly-sweet voice she always used when she wanted to impress somebody.

The thought made him angry. He grabbed the phone from Jemma.

"This is Reid. You'd better make time to talk to *me*." His voice shook so much he could barely say the words but he kept going. "Look, Monique, I know you've got Hannah. Tell me where you are so I can come and get her or I'm putting out an Amber Alert on her. You got that? Tell me! Now!"

"I won't do that," Monique said defiantly. "I'm not letting her out of my sight."

A thread of worry in her voice gave him pause. "Why not?"

"It's Rick," she said tearfully. "He's in a mood because I made the mistake of telling him you threatened me yesterday." She paused. "He said he was going to do something to get even with you and I was afraid he'd take it out on Hannah so I walked her out of school." She swallowed a sob. "I'm in a motel but I'm not telling you where I am. As soon as it gets dark out, I'm putting Hannah in my car and getting far away from here. Neither you nor Rick will ever threaten me again."

In a motel...

"Monique, please listen to me—"

"No, Reid, you listen to me! I tried to talk to you about coming to an agreement concerning Hannah, but you wouldn't listen to reason so I'm taking matters into my own hands."

It was clear that she planned to disappear with their child.

When we settled the divorce, she ended up with enough money to live like royalty for the rest of her life...

Reid's mind began to spin. How many motels were there in this area? Time was of the essence. He handed the phone to Jemma and whispered, "I'm going to call the police. Keep her talking."

He pulled his phone from his pocket to make the call. He wanted to explain the situation to them, asking them to check all the motels and hotels in the area until they found Monique. Before he had the chance, the phone rang in his hand. The screen read "Merrick Public Works." He pressed the phone to his ear. "This is Reid. What can I do for you?"

"This is Al Dvorak at the city garage. Say, you asked me ta give you a call if I saw that black Silverado in the parking lot. The guy just parked it and he's walkin' up the hill."

Reid's heart pounded like a jackhammer in his chest. Jeffers was forty minutes early. He'd purposely decided to show up before their meeting time to throw Alana off course...

"Okay, thanks, Al. I surely appreciate that."

Reid ended the call and turned to Jemma. "Keep talking to her and see if you can get the motel location out of her," he whispered. "If you do, call the police right away. I've got to get home right now!"

Reid dialed 911 as he ran out of the school. "Hello? I'd like to report an Amber Alert and a possible hostage situation." He just hoped the police could get to Essie's house in time to catch Rick Jeffers before he did. If Jeffers harmed Alana in any way...

The thought made him sprint to his car.

Chapter Fourteen

Alana sensed the man's presence before she saw him standing in her kitchen. The hair on her arms bristled as goosebumps covered her skin. A chill ran down her spine. Why did the alarm system fail to beep when he opened the door? Had Reid and Nate accidentally disabled it when they were setting up their equipment?

"You're early," she said slowly, trying not to sound rattled. The plan had been for her to head over to the Bakken house in a couple minutes to wait with Jemma and Hannah so Reid could surprise Rick Jeffers and trick him into a confession.

What happened to Reid? she thought helplessly. *He should have been back by now.*

Rick Jeffers' cold, dark eyes pinned her with his intense stare. "I wanted to be sure you were alone."

Her stomach flip-flopped. "Do you have the money? Ten percent down and ten percent for me?" She hoped she could keep him distracted with their business until Reid showed up.

He opened his coat and pulled out a thick envelope, dropping it on the kitchen counter. "It's all here." He gave off edgy vibes as he stood ramrod straight, his hands clenched at his sides. His voice had a harsh tone in it that she hadn't heard last time. He glanced around. "Don't think of double-crossing me."

She laughed nervously and stared at the diamond in his ear. A diamond most likely paid for with Monique's divorce settlement. "What do you mean?"

"I mean," he said as a quiet anger rose in his voice, "don't get any ideas about ripping up the paperwork after I leave and taking off with the money."

"Why would I do that?"

He moved closer. "You suddenly changed your mind about selling and now you want that extra ten percent under the table."

"What? You don't trust me?" She took a step backward. "I consider it a finder's fee. What's wrong with that? My parents never have to know about it."

He moved closer. "I don't trust anybody. Including you…"

She backed away. "Even if I did try to abscond with it, my parents would find out from you, so what's the point?" She put out her hands to create a barrier between them. "Please, stop right there."

His eyes swept the length of her body then focused on her face like a laser beam. "Why, are you afraid of me?"

She forced herself to act undaunted by his remark. "Look, let's quit the chit chat and get this over with. Did you bring the paperwork? I need to look it over carefully before I sign anything—"

A car suddenly tore into the driveway and came to a sliding stop. Rick's head jerked toward the window. He glowered. "We've got company."

Alana held her breath as Reid strode across the porch and opened the door. He stood with his hands at his side, his fists flexing.

Rick's face turned to stone. "I wondered how long it would take you to show up."

Reid stared coldly into his eyes. "You're all done, Jeffers. We're on to you—and your girlfriend."

Rick grabbed Alana by the arm and pulled a Glock pistol from a shoulder holster inside his coat. Alana stiffened as Rick's hand gripped her by the neck. "Make a move and I'll snap her like a pretzel."

Reid stood perfectly still. "Like you did to Essie? I know you killed her. I know how and I know why."

Rick uttered a derisive laugh. "You don't have proof of anything."

"Oh, yeah, I do. I've got security cameras on my backyard. I didn't know it at the time, but one of them had been hit by a branch during a storm and turned toward this yard." Reid displayed a taunting smile. "When I realized what had happened, I looked up the video from that day and saw everything. It was almost dark. You stood on the porch next to Essie. You placed your hand flat on her back and gave her a quick shove. Couldn't have been easier." Reid raised his palms. "Then, cool as a cucumber, you walked past her dying body and went back down the path to your Silverado."

Rick tightened his hold on Alana. "Nice try, Sinclair, but I'm not buying it."

"Let go of me!" Alana struggled to get away, but it only made him grip her tighter. The brutal look in his eyes made her realize he was going to kill her, too. And Reid. The thought of him getting away with even one murder, much less two more, suddenly filled her with more anger than she ever thought possible. "You killed her; I know you did," she said accusingly in a deadly whisper. "You murdered a defenseless old woman simply because she wouldn't give you what you wanted."

"So what?" Rick glared at her with indifference. "She was old. She wouldn't have lasted much longer anyway. I did her a favor."

Sirens wailed in the distance.

"The cops are on their way, Jeffers," Reid said a steely-calm voice. "Put the gun down. It's all over."

"Only for you." Rick shoved Alana toward the door. "She's coming with me."

Reid stepped closer. "Who else was the favor for? Monique? I've got news for you, buddy. It's all over for her, too. The cops are looking for her right now and when they find her, she's going to jail for kidnapping."

"I don't know what you're talking about." Rick's eyes narrowed. "She's got nothing to do with this."

"Nice try, Jeffers, but I'm not buying it," Reid said, mocking him. "She knows I'm on to her so she pulled Hannah out of school this afternoon and disappeared. She's gone."

Rick displayed a sardonic smile, as though he'd just heard the stupidest joke.

"I talked to her on the phone a couple minutes ago," Reid continued. "She said you were in a mood because she told you about our argument in the school parking lot yesterday. She was afraid you might take it out on Hannah to pay me back so she's left town without you." Reid shook his head. "She's leaving you holding the bag…"

Rick's eyes widened. His face flushed with anger as Reid's remark hit a nerve. Holding Alana in front of him, he backed into the screen door and pushed it open at the same time leveling his gun at Reid's chest.

She had a choice to make; either allow him to drag her away or take a stand and fight. She chose to fight. She grabbed at his gun and began to struggle with him, hoping it would distract him enough for Reid to take it away. In all the excitement, she didn't realize she'd started screaming with rage.

Suddenly Nate sprang into the doorway with a garden shovel and slammed it on the back of Rick's head, knocking him out cold. The gun fell from Rick's hand and hit the floor with a thud as his legs gave way, taking Alana down with him. She fell on top of him, screaming and pummeling him, but two pairs of hands gently pulled her to her feet.

"Alana! Calm down. You're safe now." Reid wrapped his shaking arms around her and held her tight. "How do you feel? Are you all right?"

"Yes," Alana sobbed. "I'm okay, just scared out of my wits. My neck is going to have bruises from here to Tuesday."

Two squad cars with blaring sirens and flashing lights pulled up on the lawn and officers jumped out. Nate dropped his shovel and it clattered on the porch as he ran to meet them.

"We only have a moment alone and this can't wait," Reid whispered in her ear. "My heart nearly stopped when Jeffers pointed that gun at you. I was afraid I would never get to tell you that *I love you*."

She pulled back, her mouth gaping. "What did you say?"

He pulled her closer as his tender gaze melted her heart. "I love you, *Lana*. Hannah and I both do."

She smiled with pure happiness as his confession sunk in. "I think I've been in love with you ever since the first time Jeffers showed up and you ran all the way over here to make sure I was okay. When you put your arms around me, I almost melted."

He prefaced his reply with an eager, passionate kiss. "If he had hurt you, I would have never forgiven myself."

She laughed. "I'm fine, but I think he's going to have a heck of a migraine when he wakes up."

"I never meant for things to get so far out of control," Reid confessed. "I'd planned to get back here and make sure you were safe and sound at Jemma's place before Jeffers arrived, but when I got to the school and Hannah was missing, everything went haywire."

Alarmed, Alana pulled away again. "Oh, my gosh, Reid. Hannah is really missing? I thought that was just a line to get Jeffers distracted. What are we doing standing here? We need to find her!"

"She was with Monique, but now she's safe," Nate said, coming up the porch steps. Two uniformed officers followed him. "I just asked these officers about her and they said Hannah is sitting in the back of a squad car right now, asking a million questions."

Everyone laughed, but Alana knew it was their way of relieving tension now that the worst was over. "What happened?"

"Jemma called me while I was monitoring the equipment in the garage," Nate continued. "She kept Monique talking until the cops found the motel Monique had taken Hannah to and arrested her." He grinned. "I'm pretty proud of the way she kept that woman from panicking and simply taking off."

Reid smiled appreciatively. "If anyone could keep Monique from hanging up, it would be Jemma."

Nate stared down at Jeffers, now groaning in pain as the officers handcuffed him. "That was pretty clever how you got him to confess to Essie's murder. And the best part? Got it all on video."

Epilogue

Mid-December

The multi-colored lights on Grandma Essie's fully decorated Christmas tree twinkled brightly. Alana stood back and admired her work. "How does that look to you, Reid?"

A robust fire crackled in the fireplace. Nat King Cole's velvety voice filled the air as Reid reached up and straightened the star on the top. "There. Now it's perfect." He moved next to her and whispered in her ear. "Hey, have I told you lately how much I love you?"

She gazed into his bright blue eyes. "Yes, you have, about five minutes ago."

"It's been that long, huh?" Lifting her chin, he lowered his mouth to hers and kissed her deeply. The moment their lips met, his arms slid around her waist, pulling her close. "It feels so good to hold you, to kiss you," he said huskily. "I love you, Alana."

Her smile welled up from her heart. "I love you so much, Reid. And Hannah." She held up her left hand and gazed at her sparkling marquis cut diamond engagement ring. Reid had surprised her with it two days ago with the excuse he couldn't wait two more weeks until Christmas to give it to her. "My life has changed so much in the last four months. I couldn't be happier."

He began to guide her in a slow, gentle waltz to the music. "This is going to be the best Christmas I've ever had. You and Hannah make my life complete. I couldn't ask for a better gift."

"What about Simon?" She chuckled. "And Dusty…"

Hannah stirred where she'd fallen asleep on the living room sofa. On the floor next to a pile of wrapped gifts under the tree, Dusty lay pouting with a large cone fastened around her neck, recuperating from getting spayed. Alana had fastened a red velvet bow on the cone to give her a little Christmas cheer, but she was having none of it.

Last week, Alana had attended two closings, one on her condo and the other on this house. She'd learned there was a waiting list for people wishing to buy the units in her building and she'd sold the condo completely furnished for a ridiculous price. She'd made enough money to not only pay cash for Grandma Essie's house, but to pay off all her outstanding bills and save some, too.

Richard Jeffers had pleaded guilty to murder and was awaiting sentencing. Monique had become a cooperating witness and admitted Jeffers had confessed Essie's murder to her the day before he'd planned to meet with Alana. It was the principal reason she'd left him and planned to run away with Hannah. She swore she'd feared not only for her own life, but Hannah's as well. She'd been granted leniency for her testimony and had received probation instead of prison time for abducting Hannah. No one, not even Jemma, had heard from her since that time.

Reid tightened his arms around Alana and kissed her again. A timer sounded in the kitchen. "Sounds like the lasagna is done." He drew in a deep breath. "Boy, that smells good. What time are we expecting Jemma and Nate for dinner?"

"The lovebirds?" Alana laughed. Nate and Jemma had been inseparable since the day they met. "They were supposed to be here ten minutes ago, but they're running late."

Tonight, Alana and Reid were celebrating their engagement and had invited Nate and Jemma for dinner. Alana went into the kitchen to pull out the lasagna and set it on the stove to cool. With all the time she'd had on her hands in the last couple months, she'd gone through Grandma Essie's favorite cookbooks and learned to make some of the recipes.

Reid followed close behind. "I hope they get here soon. I'm starving."

Alana held up one of Grandma Essie's Fostoria crystal serving plates, a housewarming gift from Terra. "Have a frosted Christmas cookie to tide you over. I made them this afternoon."

Reid grabbed two. "Don't mind if I do." He bit into one. "These make me feel like a kid again."

"Enjoy it while you can." Alana set the plate back down on her new granite countertop. "I won't have as much time to play around with cooking and baking once I go back to work."

Chad had finally landed the job at Rockwell and after five separate interviews, Alana had become his first team member with a starting date of January 10th. She'd negotiated a signing bonus and a higher salary than her last job, but best of all, she had a flexible schedule so she could work from home two days a week—her huge, new home in Merrick, Minnesota.

She went into the dining room to check the place settings and make sure she hadn't forgotten anything. In the center of Grandma Essie's oak pedestal table, Alana had placed a three-candle centerpiece made with balsam and white pine pieces, pinecones and holly berries. The pine scented decoration was a congratulatory gift from her college ex-roommates to celebrate her new job—and her new love.

She gazed at the pretty arrangement and thought about that balmy night in Paris where she, Josie, Ryley, Emma and Annika had made a bet in the form of a promise to each other to swear off men for one year so they could focus on pursing their professional goals instead.

She laughed.

Sometimes the best bet is the one you lose…

The End

A note from Denise...

Thank you so much for reading *Unfinished Business* and being supportive of my work! If you'd like to know more about me or my other books, you can visit my website at:

www.deniseannettedevine.com

Sign up for my newsletter at:

http://eepurl.com/csOJZL

and receive a free romantic suspense novella!

Like my Facebook page at:

https://www.facebook.com/deniseannettedevine

or...

Join my private group exclusively for sweet romance:
https://www.facebook.com/groups/HEAstories/

More Books by Denise Devine

Christmas Stories – only 99 cents

Merry Christmas, Darling

A Christmas to Remember

A Merry Little Christmas

Once Upon a Christmas

~*~

A Very Merry Christmas (Hawaiian Holiday Series)

153

Denise Devine

Bride Books – all available on Kindle Unlimited

The Encore Bride

Lisa – Beach Brides Series

Ava – Perfect Match Series

Other Books

This Time Forever - an inspirational romance

Hot Shot – a free novella

Romance and Mystery Under the Northern Lights – anthology of short stories

Recipes of Love (cookbook)

The Bootlegger's Wife – on Kindle and KU

Guarding the bootlegger's Widow – Coming Soon!

Boxed Sets on Kindle

Love, Christmas

Sweet & Sassy Cinderella

Invincible - Strong and Fearless

Invincible Secrets

Sweet and Sassy Holiday

Want more? Read the first chapter of this book and each of my most popular novels on my blog at: http://www.deniseannette.blogspot.com